WIND OF CHANGE

Cowgirls in Time Romance Series

A Chill Wind

Wind Beneath My Wings

Against the Wind

The Healing Wind

Ride Like the Wind

Wind of Change

WIND OF CHANGE

Erica Einhorn

Ralston Store Publishing
P.O. Box 1684
Prescott, Arizona 86302

ISBN 978-1-938322-29-7

Professionally and lovingly edited by:
Jennifer Hope
www.MesaVerdeMediaServices.com

Printed in the USA.

Dedicated to the one I love . . .

CHAPTER ONE

RUSH! RUSH! RUSH! Rachel was tired of leaving every-thing until the last minute, but it was something that she had always done. As frustrating as it was, it was also familiar and comfortable. And it had its advantages, after all. She didn't have to think about something until right before it needed to be done. It also had its drawbacks, though. Some things never "needed" to be done and therefore never got done. Like the chairs in her one-room schoolhouse. They were just chairs, not chair-desks. It's something she had wanted to change since she started teaching here, and look, she thought as she gazed out into the room, they are still *just* chairs—even after a year. It would be so much better for the students—and her—if there were desks that they could write on. Maybe someday, if she wasn't racing around to finish something else, she could think about getting some chair-desks for her classroom.

That wasn't now, of course. She finished sharpening the pencils and plunked the last one down on her desk. It would have been so much easier with ballpoint pens. But Josiah, Jenna's husband and the sheriff of Red Bluff, wouldn't allow her—or anyone—to bring anything into the nineteenth century that wasn't supposed to be here already. At least, nothing that would be in public view. Sarah, the saloon keeper's wife, had her iPhone, Ryan had his iPad, and even Mary Elizabeth, who was *from* the nineteenth century, had an iPhone that she loved and wouldn't give up. But everyone kept the forbidden items hidden from all but the twenty-first-century folk who lived in town. There were the composting toilets that were here and there around town, but Josiah didn't say much about them. Since they didn't require electricity, and they looked simple, he didn't think they would attract much attention. And of course his wife, Jenna, had the first one, so he couldn't say much anyway. The only ones who had a composting toilet, though—that she knew of—were twenty-first-century people, anyway.

And the town was filling up with them! Ever since Jenna had stumbled into the cave that led to the nineteenth century, she, some of her family, and some friends —including Rachel—had moved here, and all for different reasons. Jenna, Sarah, Kat, and Granny had moved here because they fell in love with a nineteenth-century man. Ryan moved here to get out of the chaos of the art store that he owned in the new Red Bluff. Rachel had moved here because, with all the cutbacks in education funding, many teachers had been laid off, and she couldn't find a job. Being a substitute teacher a day or two a week wasn't what she wanted to do. And when the previous schoolmarm, Annie—Rachel chuckled at her own nineteenth-century reference—got married and moved away, Rachel didn't hesitate to accept the position that would allow her to work full-time teaching.

Teaching in a one-room schoolhouse was a challenge,

but she enjoyed it. The children were so wonderful. Well, most of them, anyway. Little Oscar Childs was constantly causing trouble, but he did liven up the classroom. That made Rachel laugh. Because that was her way: minimize the negative, and maximize the positive. The positive was Jamie Givens. He was six years old and had more personality than ten kids. And he was a *good* kid. She had to stop herself from hugging him all the time. He was so huggable! And then there was Eugene Smythe. He had been in her classroom for a few months when she first started teaching here. Almost eighteen years old, he would sit in the front of the classroom making moon eyes at her. Although he was handsome, he was so young! Not that she was that much older, but still. It was inappropriate.

Rachel sighed. Her life was almost perfect. Almost. She loved her job and loved her life here in the nineteenth century. But she was alone and lonely. Although she hated to admit it, it was true. She wanted a man in her life. And besides young Eugene Smythe, there weren't many eligible men around. Well, there was Nick. And he had moved here from the twenty-first century for the same reason that she had: a job. He was now the deputy sheriff. But the problem was that he was from the *twenty-first century*. Now that she was comfortable and established in the nineteenth century, she wanted a nineteenth-century man. Nick was handsome and all, but he was too twenty-first-century for her.

Glancing up at the clock, Rachel smiled that she had gotten everything prepared and still had time. She was about to sit in her seat and wait for the children to arrive, when she gasped and involuntarily brought both hands to her cheeks. Rachel ran out the door, across the intersection, and then up the street toward Ralston General Store. When she opened the door and stepped in, she was breathless but happy to see Mary Elizabeth behind the counter and no sign of Ryan.

Tiptoeing to the counter, she whispered, "Did you get them?"

Mary Elizabeth had been standing with both hands on the counter. Now she picked them up to reveal what was underneath. "Here ya go, Rachel!"

From upstairs, Ryan called out, "Mary Elizabeth? Do you need any help?"

"No, I can handle it, Ryan, thank you." Mary Elizabeth smiled conspiratorially at Rachel.

Rachel grabbed the index cards from the counter and stuffed them inside her shirt. "Thank you so much, Mary Elizabeth! Josiah has everybody on edge with his rules for 'how a twenty-first-century person should act in the nineteenth century.' They're just index cards—criminy!"

"I bought plain ones; I figured they would be more acceptable." Mary Elizabeth stifled a laugh.

"How much do I owe you?"

"Nothing! I bought them at the dollar store! They're my gift to you for giving me a fun, clandestine activity! It gave me an idea for my next novel!" Mary Elizabeth looked at the clock. "You better hurry now, Rachel! It's almost time for school!"

Rachel glanced up said, "Oh!" and ran for the door. Then she turned around and said, "Thank you, Mary Elizabeth" in a quiet voice. She closed the door softly behind her and walked briskly down the street still smiling from her encounter with her friend.

CHAPTER TWO

NICK LOOKED UP as Rachel raced by the sheriff's office window. He glanced at the clock and laughed. Rachel always left everything until the last minute. Almost every day she'd rush by at this time, on her way to or from Ryan's store. You'd think she would have learned by now. But the truth was, he enjoyed seeing her. She always had a smile on her face, and that made him smile. And that was good.

There was something appealing about her, and it wasn't just her smile. He loved her long hair and found her very pretty. And her bubbly personality attracted him. Although he didn't know her very well—besides seeing her occasionally when they were growing up years ago, he had seen her a few times in Ryan's store and run into her a time or two at the local saloon—he thought he might want to get to know her better. No; he shook his head and frowned. She was a twenty-first-century girl. And now that he lived in—and loved—the nineteenth century, he wanted a nineteenth-century girl. Not that there were any in town—but that could change anytime. Yes, Rachel was pretty, but she wasn't the girl for him.

He went back to his book, but he couldn't get her off his mind. Again and again, he would picture her hurrying by, trying to make it back to school on time. And again and again, it would make him smile, as he was now, the book fallen from his hands and him gazing stupidly out the window like a schoolboy. Wouldn't this be a great time for—yup, the door opened and Josiah strode in.

"Hey, Nick. How was the night?" Before Nick had a chance to answer, Josiah said, "And why do you have that stupid grin on your face? It must be a woman!"

Without answering, Nick scowled, picked up his book, and moved to the chair beside the desk, so Josiah could take his customary seat. He didn't want to get into this with Josiah; and he especially didn't want Josiah's wife, Jenna, to find out that he found Rachel attractive. She'd be inviting them both over for supper before he could even say that although he thought Rachel was pretty, she wasn't the girl for him. So it was better not to answer at all.

"What gives, Nick? You giving me the silent treatment?" There were some wanted posters on the desk, and Josiah began glancing through them.

"Everything was fine last night. No excitement." Before Josiah could ask a question that Nick didn't want to answer, Nick stood up. "I'm going to the store. Be back soon. Bye."

He slipped out the door and walked next door to the Ralston General Store, owned by Ryan, his best friend. Opening the door, he smiled when he saw who was behind the counter. "Mary Elizabeth! Good morning! Is your groom around today, or is he—*away*?" Bear, their golden retriever, ran up to Nick and jumped on him.

Nick took the dog's paws and placed them on the ground. "Bear, *off*! You're getting too big to jump on people." The dog wagged his tail and smiled up at Nick until Nick bent down again to pet him.

"I'm right here, Nick!" called Ryan from the back room.

Nick smiled at Mary Elizabeth and walked to the back. Ryan sat in front of an easel with a beautiful painting of his big sorrel horse, Treetop. "Wow, Ryan! That's the best you've done yet! It makes it look like he's standing right here!"

"It's good," said Ryan, "but that one"—nodding to the picture on the wall of Mary Elizabeth—"is my masterpiece."

Nick laughed. "Yes, of course. Your bride." He pulled up a chair and sat next to Ryan. "Can I talk to you a minute, bud?"

"Sure, Nick. It sounds serious. Is everything all right?" Ryan turned to look at him.

Lowering his voice so Mary Elizabeth couldn't hear, he said, "Yeah, everything is fine. It's just—Rachel."

"Ohhhh," Ryan said in a normal voice, "you finally realized that Rachel is the girl for you, huh?"

Nick motioned quickly with his hand. "Shhhh. I don't want Mary Elizabeth to hear."

"She's working on receipts. It's taking all of her concentration. No worries." Ryan turned back to his painting and added more blue paint to the sky.

"Well, she's not the girl for me, and I don't want your sister Jenna inviting us both over for dinner. I like looking at her. That's all. She's pretty. *You* can understand that."

"You like looking at her, and that's all, huh?" Ryan stole a quick glance at Nick and returned to the painting.

"I think she's funny and has a great personality, too. That doesn't mean anything. I want a nineteenth-century girl. You can understand that, Ryan. *You* got one."

Ryan laughed. "True, but it wouldn't have made any difference to me."

"You can say that now, but she *is* a nineteenth-century girl." Nick crossed his arms on his chest.

Ryan laughed again. "Yes, but she wants to be a twenty-first-century girl!"

"Not anymore!" said Mary Elizabeth.

Nick leaned forward. "Ryan!" he whispered. "You said she wasn't listening! Now she'll tell Jenna!"

Ryan raised his voice. "Mary Elizabeth, please assure my friend Nick here that you will not tell Jenna anything that he said."

"I won't tell Jenna anything, Nick. Honest," said Mary Elizabeth.

Nick jerked his head around toward the front of the store and then jerked it back toward Ryan, frowning. Then he tightened his fists and stood up. Before he even had a chance to return the chair where he had gotten it from, he heard the front door of the store open and someone walk in.

"Hi, Papa!"

"Hallo, Mary Elizabeth!" said a deep voice that Nick recognized as Mr. Mills. "Get off me, Bear!"

Nick sighed deeply, and with slumped shoulders and hands in his pockets, he walked out from the back room. "Bye, Mary Elizabeth. Hallo and good-bye, Mr. Mills."

"Nick! Good to see you! I've been meaning to stop by the sheriff's office to see you, but I've been really busy at the bank." Mr. Mills shook his hand.

Nick brightened. "Do you need help with something?"

"No, no, nothing like that. I thought that since you and I were both Masons that we should get together. I wanted to invite you over for supper."

"Oh," said Nick, surprised.

"So? Will you come? Say tomorrow night at six o'clock?"

"I'll see if I can get Josiah to cover for me for a few hours, and if he can, yeah, sure I'll come to supper. Thank you!"

"I'm sure he will accommodate you if he knows where you'll be going," said Mr. Mills confidently. "I'll see you tomorrow at six, then!"

Nick smiled and walked toward the door. "Thanks, Mr. Mills. See you then."

"Hey, Nick!"

Nick turned back to look at him. "Yes?"

"Call me John!"

CHAPTER THREE

WHEN RACHEL RETURNED from the store, Jamie's grandparents were dropping him off. She waved to them with a big smile on her face. Little Jamie Givens came running up to Rachel and hugged her tightly. "I missed you, Miss Jenkins!" he said.

Rachel laughed. "I saw you yesterday, Jamie!"

He shrugged. "Yeah, I know. But I missed you, anyway."

She gave him another quick squeeze and ushered him into the schoolroom. Jamie Givens was the light of her life. He had the biggest brown eyes she had ever seen, with long lashes, and a round innocent face with his bangs hanging down almost into his eyes. His parents had died of the flu several years before, and his grandparents had been taking care of him. They were poor people and didn't have much, but they took good care of him. Rachel was grateful for that. She gave him a pencil and a piece of paper, and let him draw while she counted out the index cards to prepare for the day's lessons.

Soon, other students began arriving, and before she knew it, school had started. The lessons went well, Oscar

Childs behaved reasonably well, and she was able to work on reading with the younger children. Jamie read so well that he was almost ready to join the older kids. But his arithmetic still needed some work. Recess, lunch, afternoon recess . . . and in no time another school day was finished, and the children all went home. All but Jamie. His grandparents were usually on time to pick him up. That's okay, thought Rachel. She gave him the paper and pencil again so he could complete his drawing. Glancing at it, she noticed that it was really good—much more detailed than a drawing of an average six-year-old would be. She'd have to have Ryan take a look at it.

As Jamie continued drawing, Rachel cleaned up the classroom and tried to prepare for the next day's lessons. Maybe she could finally get everything prepared early and not have to run to the store in the morning. Rachel laughed thinking that would probably be a first.

"Why are you laughing, Miss Jenkins?" asked Jamie.

Rachel put her hand on his shoulder. "I'm laughing at myself, Jamie. I always leave everything until the last minute, and I was thinking that maybe this time I could be prepared early."

"Is it better that way?" He continued to draw while he asked questions.

"I don't know. Sometimes I think that it would be better." She took a closer look at the drawing. "What is that, Jamie?"

"That's town. See, here's the bank and the hotel, and across is the store and the sheriff's office."

Rachel nodded. "Yes, I do see. Your perspective is amazing. How did you learn to do that?"

"What's berspective?"

"Perspective. It's——"

The door opened, and Jamie's grandfather rushed in with a serious expression. "Miss Jenkins, I need to talk to you. Jamie, would you go out and wait with your Grammy, please?"

"Grampie!" Jamie threw his arms around the man's legs and hugged him.

"Go on, Jamie. I need to talk to the schoolmarm."

"Okay, Grampie. Bye, Miss Jenkins!" He hugged Rachel, kissed her on the cheek, and ran out the door to the wagon waiting outside.

"Miss Jenkins, my wife and I just received a telegram from my parents. They're in their sixties, and they need our help. My father has taken ill, and my mother is unable to take care of him by herself. If my mother can't find anyone to help her, we may have to leave for a couple of weeks to help her find someone. Would you be willing to take care of Jamie for a time?"

Although Rachel was flustered, she didn't hesitate to answer. "Yes, of course! I'd be happy to take care of Jamie. He's a sweetheart!"

The man smiled a tight smile. "Thank you. I was hoping you'd say that. The stage office is already closed. But we'll make arrangements tomorrow and probably leave the next day. We'll drop Jamie's clothes off then."

"Sure, that would be fine." Rachel smiled warmly at him.

He tipped his hat and started toward the door. "Thank you, Miss Jenkins." Then he walked out toward the wagon, climbed in, and shook the reins.

Rachel watched as the wagon disappeared out of sight. Taking care of Jamie Givens for two weeks! What a pleasure that would be! A frown creased her forehead.

Toys. She didn't think that Jamie had many, and she would like to keep him happily occupied while he was with her. But she wouldn't have time before his grandparents left to go to the new Red Bluff to pick up any toys for him. Maybe Ryan had some toys at the store. Since she had never looked, there was a chance.

After racing up the street as she did most mornings, she charged into the store. When she looked up, she saw Ryan, Mary Elizabeth, and Nick at the front counter. Bear ran up to her. She kneeled down to pet him before he could jump up on her.

"It's already after school, Rachel. What's your hurry this time of day?" Ryan put his hands on his hips and looked at her with a smile.

Rachel shook her head and laughed. "Am I getting a reputation now?"

Ryan said, "No," while at the same time, Nick said, "Yes."

And that made Rachel laugh some more. "I'm looking for some toys. Do you have any?"

"Toys? What are you *teaching* in that school of yours?" asked Ryan.

"It's not for teaching. You know Jamie Givens, the six-year-old in my class? His grandparents are leaving town for a couple of weeks, and I'm going to take care of him. I just wanted something to keep him busy—you know, something that would be appropriate for the nineteenth century."

"We don't have any toys here now, Rachel. Sorry. Can you go *there* to get some?" asked Mary Elizabeth.

"I would, but I don't have time. They're leaving in a couple of days."

Nick shrugged. "I'm free during the day. I can go

13

tomorrow and pick up some toys for you."

"Really, Nick? Would you do that?" Rachel looked at him hopefully.

"Sure, it's nothing. I like toy stores. This just gives me an excuse." Nick smiled at her and looked away.

"Nick," said Ryan sternly, "nothing that's electrical. Only toys that would be *appropriate* in this century. No exceptions. Really."

"Man, you're getting as bad as Josiah. I know the drill, okay? No electronics and nothing electric. Got it, boss!" Nick saluted Ryan and clicked his heels together.

"Thank you so much, Nick. I really appreciate this. Now I have to run home and get my house ready for a six-year-old!" Rachel hurried toward the door.

"Good luck," called Mary Elizabeth as Rachel stepped outside.

CHAPTER FOUR

WHEN JOSIAH CAME in the following morning, Nick reported that nothing had occurred the night before, and he said good-bye. He wanted to get to the new Red Bluff early so he could return with the toys for Rachel. Walking down toward the livery, he only regretted not being able to see Rachel run by as she did most mornings. For some reason, he always looked forward to that. It wasn't that he liked her or anything—at least not as a man likes a woman—but he just enjoyed watching her. There was nothing wrong with that.

Ezra, the liveryman, was cleaning a front stall when Nick walked in. "Hi, Nick. I fed them early like you asked. Would you like me to get them ready for you?"

Nick laughed. "You always ask, Ezra, and I always say no. Don't you get tired of asking?"

Ezra smiled and leaned on the pitchfork he used to clean the stalls. "It's my job, man. And maybe someday you might change your mind. Who are you going to ride today?"

"I don't know yet. Let me talk to them so I can find out."

Ezra nodded and went back to work, as Nick walked down to the end stalls. When Nick first moved here, Ezra had put his two horses, Cisco, the bay, and Shiloh, the paint, in stalls next to each other. But they were used to being together. So Nick offered Ezra money to let him take down the partition between the stalls so the horses could be together. Ezra said it was fine if Nick would put the partition back up when he moved the horses out. Nick readily agreed and removed it.

When he opened the gate of their stall, both horses came over to nuzzle him. And he noticed that Ezra had put his brushes—which Nick kept in an old fishing box— by the stall door. The fact that Ezra thought of everything made Nick smile. Everyday, Nick would walk over to the livery and groom his horses. No one knew about that except Ezra, and he was sworn to secrecy. Nobody needed to know how much his horses meant to him. That was between him and them. And they obviously relished the attention!

"Okay, who wants to go today?" Nick asked as he stroked both horses' necks. "Do you, Cisco? Or do you, Shiloh? You know you both can't go. We have to decide. Who wants to go more?" Nick "heard" his horses talk back to him. He had never told anyone that and most likely never would. Who would believe him, anyway? But when Nick smiled and looked at both their faces, he expected an answer. And when Cisco said that it was his turn because Shiloh had gone last time, Nick knew he had his answer. Cisco was correct. Shiloh had gone last time. "Sorry, ole boy. It's Cisco's turn this time." He stroked Shiloh's neck and kissed him on the forehead.

Then he picked up the brush and started brushing Cisco's back. When he finished, after being careful to clean where the cinch goes, he put the saddle pad and saddle on—which Ezra had brought to him while he brushed. Each horse had its own saddle and saddle pad, and Ezra knew which was which. The guy was invaluable, really. He took great care of the horses, and Nick appreciated that.

He gave Shiloh one last kiss, led Cisco out of the stall, and swung on. "Bye, Ezra. We'll be back sometime this afternoon. See ya."

It shouldn't take him long to get to the new Red Bluff. That way he could spend some time perusing all the toys and still make it back in plenty of time for supper with John and Cora Mills. When he got to the turn-off trail to the cave, he heard something. Voices. Children's voices. Ten feet down the trail, hidden by a bush, were two boys heading straight for the cave.

"What are you two doing here?" asked Nick.

One of the boys shrugged. "We're going for a walk. This looked like a good place."

"Why aren't you in school?"

"There's no school today," said the boy.

Nick thought a minute. It was not the weekend, and there was no holiday that he knew of—if they even had holidays back in the nineteenth century. He shook his head. "You two are skipping school! And I will have none of that! What are your names?"

"I'm Billy Bob, and this is Bobby Bill. And you're not the boss of us."

"Right. Billy Bob and Bobby Bill. How convenient. Do you know who I am?"

"Sure," said the boy who called himself Billy Bob, "you're the drunk deputy."

Nick practically choked. "No, I *am* not! The previous

17

deputy quit his job and moved out of town. I am the new deputy, and I am *not* a drunk! And you two are in big trouble. You will turn around right now and march yourselves back to school!"

"How 'bout you give us a ride?"

"This horse would just as soon buck you off as look at you. Come on, turn around. I'll walk you back."

"You don't have to do that. We can find our own way, can't we, Bobby Bill?" He looked at the other boy, and they both giggled.

"Sure you will. Turn around now! I'll walk back with you."

The boys stepped around the horse and walked down the trail. When they got to the main road, they turned left.

"Do you think that I don't know the way?"

"Just checking," said Billy Bob.

Nick was glad that he didn't have his rope with him. Because if he did, he would be tempted to lasso the two boys and drag them back to town. It wouldn't be pretty, but it would get the job done! Now he walked behind them, and they walked very slowly. Too slowly. "Cisco? Would you hurry the boys up a little please?" Cisco nudged the closest boy in the back.

"Hey!"

"Walk faster, or I'll have him pick you up by the collar and drag you back."

"You wouldn't dare!"

"Watch me!"

"Okay, okay, we'll walk faster."

The pace was still too slow. They were walking faster, but by no means fast. And Nick not only had to get to town to get the toys, but now he realized there was another chore that couldn't be put off. Doc had mentioned it before, but no one had ever followed through. Now was the time.

"Boys, time to run. I've had it with you two. Run! Now! Or my horse will chase you down!"

The boys ran. Not fast. They obviously didn't think he would actually run them down. But they did run, and soon they were in town, and in front of the school. Nick ground tied Cisco, grabbed the boys gently around their necks, and escorted them into the school.

"Um, Miss Jenkins?" Nick said as they came through the door. "I think I found something of yours."

"Oscar! Reuben! Where have you boys been?"

"Studying," said the boy formerly known as Billy Bob.

"Yeah, right!" Rachel turned to Nick. "Thank you for returning them, Nick. I appreciate it."

"No problem, Ma'am!" Nick turned and walked down to where he had left Cisco, who was grazing on some grass. "Good boy, Cisco." He jumped into the saddle, turned the horse, rode up the street, and left him in front of Ralston General Store.

Walking in briskly, he looked for Ryan. "You've got to help me, man. Is Mary Elizabeth here?"

"She's upstairs. What do you need?" asked Ryan.

"I just found two kids on the trail to the cave. They were almost there. We need to cover up the trail and create a new, hidden one right now. It can't wait."

Ryan shook his head. "We knew we should do that, and we haven't. That was close. Thank goodness you found them before they reached the cave." He stepped around the end of the counter and into the other room. "Mary Elizabeth! You ready? I need you to take over for me for a while."

19

"I'll be down in a minute. You two go ahead!"

"Let's go," said Ryan. "Bye, Honey," he yelled upstairs.

CHAPTER FIVE

AFTER NICK LEFT, Rachel said to the two boys, "I would like you both to see me at recess."

Reuben said, "Yes, Ma'am," and Oscar just shrugged and took his seat.

Five minutes later, when Rachel had finally settled the class down from the interruption, she began her lesson. Another knock at the door. She walked across the room and opened it. Jamie's grandfather was standing at the door holding a small ragged suitcase.

"Miss Jenkins, I hope this doesn't inconvenience you too much, but we were able to get tickets for today's late afternoon stage, and we need to leave now to have time to get there. Would you mind taking the boy starting today?"

"No, not at all. That would be fine." Rachel turned back toward the class. "Let me get Jamie, so you can say good-bye."

"No! Wait! We haven't told him we're leaving." The grandfather looked away and while still looking down, said, "You know, we don't want to upset the boy."

Rachel shook her head. "But—"

The grandfather reached out and touched her hand. "It's better this way, Miss Jenkins. Trust me. It's better for everybody. Good-bye." He put the suitcase down and started walking away.

"Wait!" When he turned around to look at her, Rachel held out the suitcase and said, "Can you please drop this off at the sheriff's office for me on your way out of town? If I bring it inside now, it will disrupt my classroom even more."

"Begging your pardon, Ma'am. Yes, that will be no trouble." He picked up the suitcase, threw it in the back of the wagon, climbed in, and shook the reins.

Rachel stood there watching them drive away. When he put the suitcase in the wagon, his wife had looked at him questioningly. About to turn back around and go inside, she saw Jamie's grandmother look back with a tear-stained face. Rachel shivered. Something was going on here, and although she didn't know exactly what it was, she didn't think it was good at all. And the grandfather saying that it's better for everybody this way? What was that about? They were only going to be gone a couple of weeks. Or were they?

The morning passed quickly, and suddenly it was time for recess. When she dismissed the class, she sat at her desk with her head in her hands.

"Miss Jenkins?"

She looked up to see Reuben standing at her desk. "Yes, Reuben?"

"You told us to come see you at recess." Reuben blinked rapidly and shifted from one foot to the other.

"Oh! Yes, that's right." Rachel looked up. "Where's Oscar?"

Reuben shrugged his shoulders. "Don't know,

22

Ma'am."

"Okay, Reuben, you know that you should have been in school this morning and not walking around, right?"

"Yes, Ma'am."

"Then why'd you do it?"

"Because Oscar didn't want to go to school, and he didn't want to not go to school alone."

Rachel recognized the double negative, ignored it, and rubbed her face with one hand. "You know, Reuben, he keeps getting you into trouble. Why do you keep listening to him?"

"Because he's my best friend. That's what friends do."

Rachel nodded to him. "Okay, since you came to see me like I asked, I won't request your parents to come in." She handed him a pencil and paper. "Take these and until the end of recess, keep writing, 'I will not skip school.' And then at afternoon recess, stay inside and do the same."

"I can do that, Ma'am, but it's not the truth. If Oscar asks me again, then I'll go. I can't let him go by himself." Reuben looked at her with clear blue eyes.

Rachel shook her head, looked at him, and tried to suppress a smile. Honor among thieves. "Just go ahead and write it, Reuben. Sit in the back of the room for now. Before you start, go outside and tell Oscar to come see me."

"I can tell him, Ma'am, but he won't come in," said Reuben, turning to go.

"How do you know?"

"Because when you dismissed us for recess, he said to me, 'I ain't a gonna see her.' And then he turned and ran outside."

"Okay, thank you for telling me, Reuben. I'll get him

23

myself." Rachel sighed and stood up, only then realizing that Jamie Givens was standing to the side, patiently waiting for her.

"Miss Jenkins? Did I hear my grandfather outside?" he said, looking up at her expectantly.

Oh, dear, she thought. She was hoping that she didn't have to do this until after school. But here he was asking the question that she couldn't lie to. "Yes, Jamie. Your grandfather was here."

"Oh. Okay," he said and turned to walk back outside.

Rachel bit her lip, stood up, and followed him out. She got to the door in time to see Oscar running after another boy, and before she could call him, Oscar tackled him hard. "Oscar! You know better than that!" Luckily, the other boy wasn't crying, but naughty little Oscar was laughing at him. "Come here, right now!" she called.

Oscar walked up to her as if nothing at all had happened. "Yeah? What?"

"You were supposed to come see me at recess, young man!"

He put his hands on his hips. "I didn't want to!"

Rachel took a deep breath to calm herself. Back here in the nineteenth century, it was permissible to slap or even hit children. It wasn't her way, but she took another deep breath to control herself. This kid, she thought, this one kid, was the only one who tested her resolve. She took him by the arm and walked him into the room far enough away from Reuben that he couldn't make eye contact unless he turned around. "You sit here." She sat him in the chair, walked to her desk to retrieve pencil and paper, returned and gave it to him. "Write 'I will not skip school' over and over until recess is over. And please tell your parents that I will need to see them."

"They won't come in," said Oscar, taking the pencil from her.

"And why won't they?"

"Because they don't care what I do. They just don't care." He said it without emotion, as if he were stating a fact, which he probably was. There were parents like that in the nineteenth century just as there were parents like that in the twenty-first century.

"Just tell them, okay?"

"Yeah, sure."

Rachel sighed again and returned outside to check on the boy who had been tackled. He was already up and around and playing with the other children. Jamie Givens was sitting under a tree with his book. She should feel elated that she would be spending the next two weeks with him, but with the odd way that his grandfather had acted, Rachel had a feeling of dread wash over her.

CHAPTER SIX

SEVERAL HOURS AFTER Nick and Ryan began disguising and filling in the old trail and creating a new, less defined trail with several fake dead ends, they returned to the store. When they came through the door, both of them hot and sweaty, the first thing that Nick did was pull his shirt over his head. "That was hot work! Thank you so much for helping, Ryan. I couldn't have done it without you!"

"No problem, Nick. It's something we all need to be concerned about." Ryan walked up to Mary Elizabeth who stood behind the counter, and said "Hi, Sweetie." Then he kissed her on the lips. "Don't hug me, though. I'm sure I stink." He looked around the store to make sure they were alone. "That's one convenience that I really miss: a shower."

"I agree. Hasn't anyone come up with a solar shower yet?" Nick wiped his neck with the shirt that he had taken off.

"Not that I know of, but that's something to think about." Ryan removed his shirt. "I'll see you later, Nick. I'm going upstairs to change."

"Yeah, I'm going to change, too. I still have to go to town to get those toys." He walked toward the door.

"Nick! What about supper at my folks?" Mary Elizabeth asked.

"Oh! Man! I forgot all about that!" Nick shook his head and grimaced.

"You'll have to get the toys tomorrow," said Mary Elizabeth.

"No, I can't. I told Rachel that I'd get them today. I have to."

"But—my father—"

"I don't have time right now, but could you tell him for me? I have to go. I *told* her."

Mary Elizabeth nodded her head with a strange expression. "Okay, Nick. Sure, I'll tell him. You're right. Go get the toys. Can you go to supper tomorrow night instead?"

"Yeah, sure! That would be perfect! Thanks for taking care of it for me, Mary Elizabeth." Nick walked out the door, wondering why Mary Elizabeth had such a big smile on her face. When he entered the sheriff's office, no one was there, so he opened the door to his private bedroom and began to change clothes. The front door opened, and Nick called out, "I'll be right there!"

"Just me, Nick," said Josiah.

Nick pulled the shirt over his head, tucked it into his clean pants, and walked into the office. "Josiah, I'm glad I caught you. Nobody in there, right?" He pointed to the jail cells.

"No. What's up?"

"I caught a couple of boys on the trail to the cave— brought them back to Rachel—but it was too close for comfort. You know what Doc and Zack did to the trail on the other side of the cave—made it much less obvious? Ryan and I completely rearranged the trail on this side, and now I'm not sure we can even find it again." When Josiah looked at him and blinked, Nick added, "Just kidding. But it's well hidden now. I have to run into town, but if I take you there on my way, will you spread the word for those who need to know?"

"Sure. We've all been meaning to do that, and we got lucky that you caught those kids. Do you know what their names were?"

"Reuben and Oscar."

"Oh, no! That would have been horrible. Oscar is trouble waiting to happen. If he had made it over 'there,' it would have been disastrous." Josiah opened the door. "I'll go get my horse and be right back."

Ten minutes later, they were on the new trail. "Do you think it's camouflaged well enough?" Nick led the way down the narrow trail.

"I think it's camouflaged too well! I'm not sure *I* can find it again!" Josiah laughed from behind. "Ah, here we are. Okay, I hope I can find my way back!"

"I hope you're kidding, Josiah." Nick turned in the saddle to look at him.

Josiah smiled. "Don't worry, I think I can figure it out. I'll see ya later." He turned his horse around and walked in the other direction.

"Bye, Josiah." Nick walked through the cave, came out on the other side, and caught his breath. The difference between the sky in the old Red Bluff and the sky in the new Red Bluff was amazing. The new Red Bluff was not that big of a city, and yet he now realized there was air pollution. He had never noticed it before. It made him feel grateful that he had decided to move to the old Red

Bluff.

He couldn't be happier there—well, he supposed he could be happier if he had a woman. And when an image of Rachel popped up into his mind, he forcefully pushed it aside. No, he thought, not *that* woman. A nineteenth-century woman! There were none, of course, but the stage was coming, and he hoped they would bring more people—preferably attractive, single-female people.

The gate for Jenna's twenty-first-century ranch—currently occupied by her niece Madison and Madison's boyfriend, Zack—was up ahead, and it made him forget about Rachel for the moment. When he came to the barn, he took the bridle off Cisco and made sure that he had water. Zack's truck was parked, but Madison's car was gone. Zack might be home, or he might have driven to college with Madison. So Nick knocked on the door of the house and waited. If Zack wasn't home now, he'd wait to leave the note about the new trail until later. No answer. Nick hopped in his truck, which was parked in what looked like a parking lot—all the people who had moved to the old Red Bluff left their cars there. Luckily they were mostly hidden from the street by a heavy growth of underbrush.

Soon he was pulling into the big parking lot of Toys'R'Us. When Nick walked in, a big smile spread across his face. If little Jamie Givens could see this place, Nick thought, he would explode with wonderment. Eagerly, Nick walked up and down the aisles to find what would be appropriate for Jamie and what would pass Ryan's approval. Anything electronic was out, so Nick walked right by those aisles without even looking. A ball? Would Ryan think a ball was all right? Maybe. If not, he could return it. He put one in the cart.

Then he found an aisle with all wooden toys. Perfect, thought Nick! The first toy that caught his eye was a train set made out of wood. The tracks fit together with snaps, but he thought that would probably pass. Next he found a dump truck with a movable back. Great! Then he found an airplane with no moving parts. He was about to put it into the cart when he realized there were no planes in the nineteenth century. Nick laughed to himself and looked around. Then he realized there were no trucks, either. Reluctantly he pulled the truck out of the cart and returned it to the shelf. Farther down the aisle, he found a big wooden barn filled with wooden farm animals. Smiling to himself, he put it in the cart.

That was probably enough, but he wanted to see what else they had—in case Jamie needed more toys later. Nothing caught his attention until he came to the sports section. Picking up a glove and sliding it on his hand, he punched the pocket gently with his fist. He thought how cool it would be to teach Jamie Givens to play baseball—no one had to know what they were doing. Pulling the glove off his hand, he was about to reach for a glove more Jamie's size when he stopped. Jamie Givens was not his kid. He wasn't even Rachel's kid—not that it made a difference. But playing baseball with somebody else's kid was not what he wanted to do. Someday, if he ever met someone he could fall in love with, he'd like to have his own son. Someday.

CHAPTER SEVEN

ALTHOUGH RACHEL SINCERELY loved teaching, at the end of each day, she was ready to go home and relax. Not on this day, though. Jamie Givens not only did not know that his grandparents were leaving, but he didn't know they had already left. They didn't want to upset the boy? So let her do it. What were they thinking? Rachel shook her head and looked up. "Class dismissed!" She waited until the sound of stomping shoes subsided before standing up and walking slowly to the door. Jamie always waited patiently just outside the door for his grandparents to pick him up. Approaching him, she said, "Jamie, come back inside, will you?"

He turned to look at her. "Sure, Miss Jenkins."

She closed the door behind them, sat down on a chair in the back of the classroom, sat Jamie down across from her, took his hands, and looked into his eyes. "Jamie, I have to tell you something." He nodded. "Jamie, your Grammy and Grampie had to go away for a while to take care of your great-grandparents."

"Are they coming back?"

When Rachel nodded, why did she have the funny

feeling that she was lying? "They said they would be back in a couple of weeks."

Tears started at the corner of his eyes. "I'll be all alone. Who's going to take care of me and bring me to school everyday?"

Rachel held out her arms and drew him into a tight hug. "Oh, Jamie! Come here! You won't be alone! I'll be taking care of you until they return!"

He blinked through the tears and looked at her. "*You'll* take care of me? Really?" When he looked up at her with his long lashes, she nearly broke into tears herself. She nodded, and he hugged her again and said, "I love you, Miss Jenkins!"

"I love you, too, Jamie." She held him away from her and said, "I need to get a few things done before we leave, and then we'll walk over to the store, buy some supplies, and stop at the sheriff's office for your clothes."

"My clothes? Aren't you staying at my house with me?"

"No, you're going to stay at *my* house with me!"

His eyes lit up. "I am? *Your* house? Wow!"

When he settled down with pencil and paper, Rachel began planning for the following day. There would be no running to the store in the morning anymore—not with a six-year-old to take care of. This would force her not to leave everything until the last minute. Maybe this was just what she needed. Glancing at Jamie, she thought that taking care of him was good for her, but she wondered what it would do to him that his grandparents had deserted him without even saying good-bye. First he lost his parents, then he lost his grandparents. Wait. What was she saying? His grandparents weren't gone. They would return in a couple of weeks. At least that's what they told her. She shook her head to dispel the odious thoughts.

"Let's go, Jamie!" She held out her hand for him. He grabbed it and smiled up at her.

They walked up the street, hand in hand, and talked about their school day. When she reached the Ralston General Store, she opened the door, and they walked inside. Mary Elizabeth was behind the counter. "Hallo, Mary Elizabeth! I'd like you to meet my new roommate, Jamie Givens. Jamie, this is Mary Elizabeth Leyton."

"Hallo, Mrs. Leyton."

"Hallo, Jamie! What a cutie you are! Would you like a piece of candy?" Mary Elizabeth stuck her hand in a jar of peppermints on the counter.

Jamie looked up at Rachel, and when she nodded, he smiled and said, "Yes, please!"

She handed him the candy and said, "Would you like to look around the store, Jamie?"

"Can I, Miss Jenkins?"

"Of course, Jamie, go ahead. Don't touch anything, though." Rachel smiled at him.

"When did this happen?"

"Oh, Mary Elizabeth, it's a long story." Rachel sighed. "His grandparents who take care of him will be out of town for a while."

"Listen, Rachel, I wanted to invite you over to supper at my parents' tomorrow night. Ryan and I will both be there. What do you think?"

"Thank you, Mary Elizabeth, but I have him." She nodded toward Jamie.

"Isn't there someone who could take care of him for you? It'll just be a couple hours or so." Mary Elizabeth looked disappointed.

"I don't know who that would be. And I don't want to leave him with a stranger. You know—"

Mary Elizabeth frowned and looked down. "Yes, I understand. Okay." She sighed. "Was there something you needed?"

After Mary Elizabeth brought her all the items on her list, Rachel dropped the coins into her hand and smiled at her. "Thank you so much for everything, Mary Elizabeth."

"No problem, Rachel. If you change your mind—"

Rachel nodded. It would have been nice to have dinner out, she thought. Opening the door, she said, "Jamie, let's go now." He ran to her and grabbed her hand.

As they walked outside, Josiah came out of the sheriff's office. "Sheriff Josiah!" Jamie said.

Josiah opened his arms, and Jamie flew into them. "Hallo, my man! How are you doing today?"

"You two know each other?" asked Rachel.

"We sure do, don't we, young fella?"

Jamie turned his head and looked at Rachel. "Sheriff Josiah is my friend!"

"I see that," said Rachel. An idea occurred to her. "Josiah, any chance you would be willing to watch him for a couple hours tomorrow evening?"

"Sure! I'd love to! I was going to stay late tomorrow night, anyway. I was just going to tell Jenna. Would you mind me bringing him over there with me? I'll bring him right back. His suitcase is in there." Josiah motioned over his shoulder into the sheriff's office. "I'll be right back."

Josiah knelt down and let Jamie climb onto his back. It looked as natural as if they had done it a hundred times. Rachel watched as Josiah walked across the street to the hotel, and then she turned and walked back into the store.

"Mary Elizabeth! Mary Elizabeth!"

Mary Elizabeth came out from the back room. "Yes? What's up, Rachel?"

"I *can* go tomorrow night. What time should I be there?"

"Ryan and I will pick you up with the wagon at 6:00."

"Great! See you then!"

"Wait! Rachel, what happened with Jamie? Where is he?"

"It turns out that he knows someone in town after all. Apparently he and Josiah are old friends."

"Oh. Jamie is the boy whose parents died of the flu a few years ago? I think Josiah took care of him for a few days after it happened."

"You weren't in town yet, were you, Mary Elizabeth?"

She shook her head. "No, but you know," she shrugged, "it's a small town."

"That it is," said Rachel. "That it is."

She walked out of the store, down a few steps to the sheriff's office, and put her hand on the door. Before she opened it, she saw Nick through the window. He was sitting at Josiah's desk reading a book, and he looked up when he heard the door rattle. For an instant, their eyes met. Rachel couldn't look away—not that she wanted to anyway. His dark eyes drew her in like a magnet. She felt her heart beat faster, and it broke her concentration. What was that about, she wondered as she opened the door and strolled in.

CHAPTER EIGHT

WHEN NICK HEARD a sound at the door, he looked up, met Rachel's eyes, and couldn't look away. Their eyes locked together, and he couldn't tear himself away. Then she blinked, broke the spell, and opened the door.

"Hey, Rachel."

"Hey, Nick." She smiled at him.

"I got all the toys for you. Do you want them all now?"

She thought for a minute. "No, not all. Leave one behind. How much do I owe you, Nick?"

Suddenly, his eyes couldn't get enough of her. He made a mental note to himself not to be in such close quarters again—around other people was fine—as long as he didn't have to look at her.

"Nick?"

"Oh, sorry!" He shrugged his shoulders. "Daydreaming. You know, let these toys be my treat."

"I can't let you do that! Come on, let me—"

The door opened, and Josiah and Jamie walked in, with Jamie still wrapped around Josiah's back, and both of them laughing. "Everything's all settled." Josiah looked first at Nick and then at Rachel. "And this little man is ready to go back to you, Rachel!" He undid Jamie's hands around his neck and helped the boy slide to the floor.

"That was fun, Josiah! Thanks! Hi again, Miss Jenkins!" Jamie looked up at her with love in his eyes and took her hand in both of his.

"Hey, Jamie. Have you met my new deputy? His name is Nick." Josiah glanced at Nick. "And, Nick, this is my friend, Jamie."

"Hallo, Jamie!" Nick stood up and put out his hand to Jamie.

Jamie smiled and held out his hand. "Nice to meet you, Depty Nick."

"Dep-u-ty," said Rachel.

"Deputy Nick."

"Good job, Jamie. Okay, let's go home now. We need to find a place for you to sleep." She turned with Jamie toward the door, then abruptly turned and looked at Nick.

"I'll deliver," said Nick.

"Thanks!" Rachel smiled, grabbed Jamie's suitcase, and opened the door.

"I'm taking off, too, Nick. Jenna is ready to go home. I'll see ya tomorrow." Then he ran his hand over Jamie's hair. "And I'll see you tomorrow, too, little man!"

"Bye, Josiah!" said Jamie. "Bye, Deputy Nick!"

Nick watched as Rachel and Jamie walked down the street. Standing by the window, he kept watching until they passed out of his view. He shook his head. Why didn't he just give her the toys? Why did he set himself up to be alone with her again? Yes, she was pretty, but she wasn't the girl for him. He didn't know what was going on, but he wasn't happy about it.

Turning around, he walked into his room and put the toy barn into a large backpack, and the ball into a paper sack. It was a grocery sack and not really nineteenth-century, but he thought he could get away with it for just a block. And he grabbed his coat and wrapped it around the balloon he had bought. He couldn't help himself. It would be deflated in a day or two, so no one would see it, anyway.

Smiling to himself, he bundled everything up and walked out of the office and down the street. Nick passed the saloon and heard Sarah, Matthew's wife, singing. He knew Sarah from the twenty-first century. She had moved here just after Jenna did. Then Nick passed the doctor's office, where Kat lived with her husband, the doctor. Kat was Jenna's sister. She didn't want to move here at all, until she fell in love with Doc. Everyone had moved here for love—well, everyone except for him, who had moved here to take the deputy job. And now that he thought about it, Rachel moved here for a job as well. They did have that in common. It didn't matter, though. He'd drop off the toys and return immediately to the office. No need for him to stay there any longer than he had to.

When he reached Rachel's house, across the street from the school, he knocked on the door. A minute later, little Jamie Givens opened the door with wide eyes.

"Hallo, Depty Nick."

"Hallo, Jamie. It's Dep-u-ty."

"Hallo, Dep-u-ty Nick."

"Hi, Jamie. Where's Rachel?"

"You mean Miss Jenkins? She's in the necessary. Do you want to come in? What are you carrying?"

Nick stepped into the house with all his bundles. "I'll let Miss Jenkins tell you what all this is."

Jamie closed the door behind Nick. "You want to see my room?"

Nick smiled at the boy. "Sure."

Jamie took Nick by the hand and led him into what they would call in the twenty-first century, a great room, which was common in the nineteenth century. The large wood cooking stove close to the center of the room served to heat the house and cook the meals. Then Jamie turned off into a side room. "See? It's all mine! My own room!"

They stood there holding hands, just inside the doorway, as Nick looked around. The room had a single bed, a bedside table, a dry sink with a bowl of water and a pitcher, and a chamber pot in the corner. It looked like nineteenth-century hotel rooms that he had seen.

"Hey, boys!"

"Hi, Miss Jenkins. I was showing Deputy Nick my room."

"Hi, Rachel," said Nick, smiling.

"Hey, Nick. Thanks so much for bringing—you know. Let's go in the other room and see what Nick has brought for you, Jamie."

"For me?"

"Yup! For you, partner!" Nick swung Jamie easily up onto his back. They walked back into the kitchen area where Nick had left his bundle, covered by his jacket, which was elevated slightly off the ground.

"What's that?" asked Jamie, squeezing Nick tightly by the neck.

"I'll show you if you let go," whispered Nick, pulling Jamie off as the boy released his neck. Then he reached under the elevated coat, pulled out a helium balloon, and held it out to Jamie.

Jamie, not yet reaching for the floating object, said, "What is it, Deputy Nick? Will it hurt me?"

"Nick!" Rachel whispered into Nick's ear. "That isn't exactly nineteenth century. What will Josiah and Ryan say?"

"It's called a balloon, Jamie. Here, take it. It won't hurt you. I promise." Then Nick turned to Rachel and said softly, "It will only float for a day or two, so neither of them should ever see it."

Jamie put his hand tentatively out and grasped the string, but when Nick let go and the balloon pulled upward, Jamie gasped and let it go. He looked at Nick guiltily. "Sorry, Deputy Nick."

Nick mussed up Jamie's hair with his hand. "No worries, little man." He knelt down beside the boy so he could look him in the eyes. "I'm the deputy sheriff, right?" Jamie nodded. "And it's my job to protect the people, right?" Jamie nodded again. "And aren't you one of the people? So if it's my job to protect *you*, I wouldn't do anything to hurt you, right?"

Nick stood up, grabbed the balloon by the string from where it had come to rest on the ceiling, and knelt back down to Jamie. "Come on, we'll hold it together, okay?" Jamie reluctantly put his hand below Nick's on the string. "Okay, hold on now. I'm going to let it go for just a second—but you hold onto it, okay?" Nick released the string and grabbed it again immediately. "Was that okay?" Jamie nodded again. "Want to try it for a little longer this time?" A hint of a smile appeared on Jamie's face when he nodded yes. Nick let the string go and counted, "one, two, three," and grabbed it again.

This time, Jamie jumped up and down. "Me, me! I want to do it alone now!"

Nick let the string go and stood up, smiling. Jamie pulled the balloon down to him then let it go up again, as he held onto the string the whole time. Then he took off running through the house with the balloon bobbing behind him. Nick looked at Rachel, and she was staring at him with her mouth hanging open. It looked funny, but it was her eyes that captured him. Again. And he couldn't look away.

CHAPTER NINE

RACHEL HAD BEEN impressed when she walked up behind Jamie and Nick and saw them holding hands. There was something about that image that touched her heart. But when she saw how patient Nick was when Jamie was afraid of the balloon, it absolutely stunned her. She had never thought of Nick as a touchy-feely kind of guy. And here he was being so incredibly kind to this little boy whom she loved so much. She didn't even realize that her mouth was hanging open until Nick looked at it, but then he focused on her eyes. And she looked back at him, as captivated as he was.

Then Jamie ran by with the balloon between them and broke the spell. Rachel watched Nick blink and then turn toward Jamie and hold out his arm to stop him. "Whoa, little man, whoa. I have to tell you something."

Jamie stopped in front of him still bobbing the balloon by the string. "Yes, Deputy Nick."

"You like this balloon, don't you?"

"Yes, Deputy Nick."

"Well, I'm glad you're having fun with it, but balloons don't last very long. In a day or two, it's going to sink to the floor and not get up again."

"Why?"

"Because that's just how balloons are. You know how cats meow and dogs bark? That's just how cats and dogs are. And that's how balloons are. They don't last very long. I wanted you to know so you it wouldn't disappoint you when it fell to the floor. Okay?"

"Okay. Are you going to take it away now?"

Nick kneeled down to look into Jamie's eyes. "No, Jamie. You can have it. But I have a couple other toys that you might like and that will last a lot longer. How about that?"

"Can I see them?"

"Sure. Come on."

Jamie released the balloon and let it float to the ceiling. Then he followed Nick to where he had left the backpack and grocery sack. Nick removed the ball from the bag and bounced it on the wooden floor.

"Jamie, what do you think of this? Isn't it cool?"

"Can I try?"

"Sure."

"Wait a minute, boys. Jamie, be careful where you bounce that ball. We don't want to break anything in the house, okay?" Rachel stood with her hands on her hips watching as Jamie bounced the ball too hard and it escaped behind him.

"I'll try to be careful, Miss Jenkins." Jamie bounced the ball into the other room and then bounced it all the way back again.

"Nick, I appreciate it, but these weren't the kind of toys that I was looking for."

"I know that. These were just extras. I have a really good one in the backpack that I think you'll approve of."

43

He turned to Jamie. "Hey, little man. Come here. I have something else for you."

Jamie dropped the ball and ran over to Nick. "More, Deputy Nick?"

Nick knelt down and pulled the wooden barn out of the backpack. "I think you're going to like this, Jamie."

"What is it?"

"Let's take it into your room, so we don't mess Rachel's house up, okay?" Nick picked up the barn with one arm and Jamie with the other, and carried them both into Jamie's bedroom. Then he put both down and opened the box with the barn in it. Jamie watched as Nick took out the barn, set it up, and removed all the animals from the box. When it was all laid out on the floor, Jamie looked at it with wide eyes and then threw himself in Nick's arms.

"Thank you, Deputy Nick, for bringing me these toys! Thank you!" Then he sat down in front of the barn and started moving the animals around.

Nick stood up, watched him for a minute, and then looked at Rachel. "That's more of what you had in mind, right?"

"It's perfect, Nick. Absolutely perfect." Rachel sighed when she saw how happy Jamie was with the new barn. She watched him briefly, then turned to Nick and put her hand on his arm. "Thank you for this, Nick. It means more than I can say, honestly. Thank you." Distracted by Jamie, she left her hand on his arm longer than was necessary, and when Nick glanced down, she quickly removed it.

"Well, my job is done here, Rachel. Time for me to head back and act like a deputy sheriff again. I'll see you later. Bye, little man! Hope you enjoy your toys!"

"Bye, Deputy Nick! Thank you!" Jamie barely looked up because he had a horse in each hand while his arm held a cow to his chest.

CHAPTER TEN

NICK WALKED OUT of Rachel's house and shivered, not from the cold, but from the discomfort he felt around Rachel. He shook himself like a dog shaking water off his coat. Then he briskly walked up the street toward the sheriff's office.

Putting his forehead to the window with his hands shielding the sun, he looked in and saw that the office was empty. Although, normally, no one would be waiting —they'd go out looking for him, because there weren't that many places to go. He backed away from the window and stuffed his hands in his pockets until he got to the Ralston General Store. It had the "Closed" sign on it. Nick knew that the door would probably be unlocked, but he chose not to go in that way. Instead, he walked around to the back entrance, opened the door, stepped one foot inside, and called out, "Anybody home?"

From the top of the stairs, Ryan said, "We're just finishing dinner, er, supper, Nick. We have more. Want to join us?"

Nick walked inside and to the bottom of the stairs. "No, thanks. Can I talk to you when you finish eating,

Ryan? It's important."

"Sure, Nick. I'll meet you over there. Won't be too long."

"Thanks." Nick walked out the back door and around the corner to the sheriff's office. After entering, he plopped down in the chair by the desk and exhaled sharply. He was in trouble, and he knew it. Although he didn't want to have anything to do with Rachel, he couldn't stop looking at her, and now, he couldn't stop thinking about her, either. Why did he have to volunteer to bring the toys over there? Yes, he spent most of the time playing with Jamie—who was a cute kid and fun to be around—but the whole time he was there, he was infinitely aware of Rachel's presence. When she put her hand on his arm, it was all he could do to stop himself from grabbing her and kissing her.

And he wasn't even interested in her! Well, that wasn't exactly honest. He didn't *want* to be interested in her. He wanted a nineteenth-century girl, and he wasn't ashamed for wanting that. He lived in the nineteenth century now —he couldn't see leaving in the foreseeable future—and so he wanted a nineteenth-century girl. That made sense, didn't it?

Ryan opened the door and walked inside, interrupting his thoughts. "So what's so important, Nick? Woman trouble?" Ryan laughed.

Nick stood up. "Not funny, Ryan. It's serious." He walked toward the door. "Come on. Let's walk."

When they were outside and heading around the corner, Nick broke the silence. "I'm in trouble, Ryan, and I don't know what to do."

"What's wrong, Nick? Is it something I can help you with?" Concerned, Ryan looked at Nick.

"It's Rachel."

Ryan laughed. "It *is* woman trouble!"

"Ryan, it's not funny. I'm developing feelings for her—and I don't want to."

"Why not? I thought you wanted a woman."

Nick shook his head. "Yes, I do, but not *that* woman."

"Why not? What's wrong with Rachel? She's pretty, she's funny, she's fun to be around. What exactly is wrong with her?"

Nick scowled. "She's not *from* here. She's from the twenty-first century! I want a woman from the nineteenth."

"Nick, we've been over all that before. It just worked out that way for me. I wouldn't have cared where Mary Elizabeth was from. You can't force your heart to love one woman when it wants to love another."

"I didn't say anything about *love*! It's not *love*! I just can't stop looking at her or thinking about her." Nick spoke quickly, like he was afraid for that thought to be out there.

"Nick, whatever it is, you're going to have to deal with it—and decide what to do. What about Rachel? How does she feel?"

"It doesn't matter. I'm not interested."

Ryan suppressed a laugh. "Yeah, okay, Nick, whatever you say." They walked in silence for a while. "So, what are you going to do?"

"That's what I was hoping you would tell me, Ryan. But since you haven't given me any good ideas, I can only think of one thing to do. Stay completely away from her. It's my only choice."

"It's a small town, Nick—"

"Doesn't matter. If I make up my mind to stay away

from her, I'm sure I can arrange that." He nodded his head and set his jaw. "Yeah, I can do that. I'll miss that kid, though. He's a little sweetheart."

"The kid you bought the toys for?"

"Yeah. I played with him tonight. Great kid."

"Okay, Nick, I think you have it figured out. Mary Elizabeth made apple pie for dessert. You want to come up and have some?"

"No, thanks, Ryan. I'm going back to the office and mope."

Ryan couldn't mask his chuckle. "Do what you have to do, buddy. I'll see ya later. Bye." Ryan patted Nick on the shoulder and walked back to the store.

Nick sighed and slowly turned toward the sheriff's office. After entering, he slumped down in the chair by the desk and grabbed a pile of wanted posters. He'd look at each one and read the information on it, but all he could see was Rachel's smile and Rachel's eyes. Frustrated, he groaned and threw the posters across the room. Exhaling quickly, he shook his head and frowned. He reluctantly stood up, picked up the posters, straightened them out, and put them back on the desk. Then he put his head in his hands and sat there for the longest time feeling sorry for himself.

CHAPTER ELEVEN

AFTER NICK LEFT, Rachel sat on the floor with Jamie to play with the barn animals. An hour later, Jamie put his hand on his stomach and looked up at Rachel. "I'm hungry, Miss Jenkins."

Rachel laughed and put her hands to her face. "Me, too! I forgot all about dinner!"

"You mean supper, right? We already ate dinner."

Rachel laughed again. "Yes, Jamie, you're right. I mean supper." As she stood up, she thought about how easy supper would be if they lived in the twenty-first century. Order pizza or Asian food to be delivered, or a TV dinner, or stick leftovers in the microwave. Ah, what she would give for a microwave about now.

Going out the back door and bringing in some kindling, Rachel started a fire in the big wood cooking stove. The rest of the evening was a blur to her. Cooking supper, eating with Jamie, telling him a story, and putting him to bed—even though it was her first time with him, it was like she did it all by rote.

All she could think about was Nick—how patient and kind he was with Jamie, how he played with Jamie without being asked, and how he bought the toys for her and wouldn't take any money for them. And of course his hypnotic dark eyes and his slender physique popped into her mind as well. Did she *like* him? He wasn't a nine-teenth-century man like she wanted, but did it matter? She wanted children and wanted someone good with kids—wasn't that more important? A lot more important. Yes, she had to admit it. She liked Nick Gal-lanti.

After putting Jamie to bed, she had a cup of chamomile tea to relax before bed and thought more about Nick. What did she know about him? He had been Ryan's friend for as long as she had been Jenna's friend. Although the four of them had never played together, and Nick hadn't even remembered her—that didn't bother her. They were all different people back then. She remembered that Jenna and Ryan's parents had been afraid that Nick would be a bad influence on Ryan. Nick had grown up the typical bad boy, getting into all kinds of minor trouble, that somehow Ryan had luckily avoid-ed. Then something really bad had happened. Rachel didn't know exactly what it was, but Nick had to go to court, and it was serious. That's when everything changed. Nick was on his best behavior after that, had whatever it was expunged from his juvenile records, and after college had immediately gone to the Police Acade-my. Now he wasn't a bad boy anymore. Now he was a good guy. And she liked him. That was her last thought before she fell asleep.

The following morning, she was awakened by Jamie jumping up and down on her bed. "It's morning, Miss Jenkins! Time to get up! I want to go to school!"

Rachel reached up and pulled him down to her, hugging him. "You're awesome, you know that?"

"Miss Jenkins, is Deputy Nick your boyfriend?"

"No! Where would you get an idea like that?"

"Because he calls you Rachel, and he brought me toys."

"All my adult friends call me Rachel. Come on! Let's get up and have breakfast."

After having breakfast and getting ready for school, they walked across the street hand in hand. While Rachel sat at her desk, Jamie sat quietly drawing on a piece of paper. Rachel realized that she didn't need anything for today's lessons. That's a first, she thought! But it was just as well. It's one thing to run down the street by herself at the last minute to get supplies from the store, but it was another thing to run down there dragging Jamie along. He was improving her life already.

The school day went on, but it was embarrassing. Several times while she was teaching, an image of Nick popped up in her mind and she lost track of where she was. More than once, a student had to say, "Miss Jenkins? Miss Jenkins!" One time, a student actually came up to the front of the room where she was and shook her. It was Oscar, of course. Who else would have the nerve and the lack of respect to do that, but Oscar? When the day finally ended, Rachel felt not only embarrassed, but confused. In the clarity of her few moments alone at recess and lunch, she had come to the determination that although she liked Nick, that didn't necessarily mean that he was the man for her.

Meanwhile the reality of being a temporary parent to Jamie was hitting her. She had forgotten to pack him a lunch, so she had to ask an older boy to run down to the hotel to bring something back for Jamie. He didn't want to, so she had to bribe him that she'd buy his dinner, too.

Lunch, dinner, supper, she still got them mixed up. And no matter how many times she tried to say otherwise, she almost always announced "lunch time" instead of "dinner time" at twelve o'clock. The kids finally didn't mention it anymore, although in the beginning, one student had told her that his father said that "lunch" was old fashioned. Then Oscar piped up and said that his father said that calling it lunch was stupid. That was in her first month of teaching, and she hadn't known how to handle Oscar yet. That delay cost her dearly, and it wasn't until much later that she could control him. Somewhat. Not that he was completely under control, even now. But he was better. And she was grateful for that.

By the time Rachel closed the school door and walked across the street with Jamie, she felt exhausted. Not exhausted from doing, but exhausted from thinking. So she was happy the hotel had sent so much food over for Jamie's lunch that there was still some left over for his supper. She didn't have to cook before bringing him over to the sheriff's office for Josiah to take care of him. And she was looking forward to eating with Ryan and Mary Elizabeth at Mary Elizabeth's parents' house. Rachel had met both of her parents, but had never had a chance to have a conversation with them. So it would be a Nick-free evening. There would be no time to think about him tonight. And she was very glad of that.

After playing with Jamie, heating his supper, and sitting with him while he ate, Rachel got dressed for her evening out. Then she and Jamie stepped out the door and walked up the street toward the sheriff's office. Rachel hoped that Nick wouldn't be there. Thoughts of him had dwindled since she left the school, and she didn't want to refresh her memory before supper.

The sight of the hotel across the street made her alter their path. "Come on, Jamie. Let's make a quick stop at the hotel first." They walked into the hotel and found Granny at the front desk.

"Who's that little cutie you have with you?" asked Granny.

"Granny, this is Jamie. Jamie, this is Granny."

Jamie looked at both women. "She's not *my* granny."

"*Everybody* calls me Granny, and you can, too! Nice to meet you, Jamie!"

"Nice to meet you, *Granny*."

Granny looked at Rachel. "Was that food that I sent over okay?"

"It was perfect! But I need more! Can I get lunch—I mean dinner—every day for the next couple weeks? And I'll have someone pick it up for me. I'm not used to having to cook three meals a day!"

"So Jamie is staying with you for a while?"

Rachel nodded. "Yes, while his grandparents are out of town. They're supposed to be back in two or three weeks."

Granny raised her eyebrows, nodded, and looked at Jamie. "Well, young man, you'll have to come visit us sometime."

"We've gotta run, Granny. Thank you!" She and Jamie turned toward the door. Then she quickly turned back around. "Oh! And I'll pay you later!"

"If you don't, I know where to find you!" Granny snickered.

They crossed the street. When they walked into the sheriff's office, and Rachel didn't see Nick, she felt relieved. Good, she thought, an evening free of thoughts of him.

"Hey there, young fella!" Josiah stood up and walked toward Jamie. "Are you ready to play something fun tonight?"

Jamie ran up to him. "I sure am, Sheriff Josiah!"

"Come on in here!" Josiah walked into the room with the jail cells. Inside the first cell was the other toy that Nick had bought for Jamie: a train track and trains that were all made out of wood. "Take a look at this!" Neither of them noticed when she slipped out the door.

When she reached her house again, Ryan and Mary Elizabeth were just turning the corner in their wagon. "Climb aboard," said Mary Elizabeth.

Ryan looked at his wife and then, with a funny look on his face, looked at Rachel. "I didn't realize that you were going with us, Rachel."

Mary Elizabeth shrugged. "I invited her."

CHAPTER TWELVE

NICK THOUGHT ABOUT whether to ride his horse or walk to supper, but finally decided on walking. There was an almost full moon, and it was a pleasant night. It wasn't that far, anyway. He arrived early, and knocked on the door.

John Mills answered. "Nick! Great to see you! So glad you could make it!" John patted Nick on the shoulder as he walked into the house.

"Thank you, John. Thanks for inviting me. It smells delicious!"

"Come on into the kitchen. Have you met my Mrs.? Cora, this is Nick. Nick, this is my wife, Cora."

"Nice meeting you, Cora."

"Nice meeting you, Nick. Go ahead and sit down. The others will be here soon." Cora turned back and stirred the pot on the stove.

"Others?" Nick looked at John.

"Oh! My daughter and her husband are coming, too. She invited herself." John shrugged.

"Ryan will be here?" asked Nick hopefully. He liked John Mills, though he didn't know much about him. But if Ryan were here, it would certainly make the evening go more smoothly.

"And a friend of Mary Elizabeth's," said Cora.

A friend, wondered Nick. Who would Mary Elizabeth bring? And then his stomach lurched and his heart raced. Before he could even say anything, he heard the door open.

"Halloooo. We're here," called Mary Elizabeth.

"There they are now. We're in here!" Cora called out.

Mary Elizabeth walked in first, followed by Rachel. Her eyes sprang open when she saw him. So she didn't know about this, either. That made Nick feel better. If he had thought that Rachel had set this up, it would have bothered him. Ryan was the last to walk in, and when he saw Nick, he looked at him and shrugged his shoulders. It wasn't Ryan's idea, either, then—he wouldn't have expected that from Ryan—but who knows. And when Mary Elizabeth glanced at Nick with a wide grin, he knew who had arranged this. Nick smiled at everyone and looked down at his hands.

"Hallo, everybody. I'm Rachel!"

"Oh, I'm sorry, Rachel. I didn't realize that you hadn't met my folks. Mama, Papa, this is Rachel. Rachel, this is my mama, Cora, and my papa, John."

Rachel nodded her head. "Nice to meet you both. Hallo, Nick."

"Rachel." He looked up briefly and smiled.

"Go ahead, everybody, sit down." Cora stirred the pot again. "This will be ready in a jiffy!"

"I'll help you, Mama." Mary Elizabeth grabbed the plates and silverware from the wooden counter and placed them on the table.

Ryan sat down next to Nick, placing his hand briefly

on his shoulder. Rachel sat down across from Nick—the worst possible place. Now he'd have to look at her all evening. And by the look on her face, she was thinking the same thing.

"Rachel is the schoolmarm," said Mary Elizabeth.

"Ah, so you're the one who took the job that should have gone to Mary Elizabeth," said John, nodding his head.

Before Rachel could speak, Mary Elizabeth said, "She saved me from the job, is more like it!"

"My Mary Elizabeth fashions herself a writer," said John almost sarcastically.

"John?" Ryan looked at his father-in-law. "You knew, didn't you, that Mary Elizabeth looked on the internet and found that she had published *several* books. She's not only a writer, she's a damn good writer!"

"Seriously?" asked John, only slightly abashed.

"Yes, Papa, seriously. *Several*. All under my maiden name, Mary Elizabeth Mills." She put down a cup of tea in front of him sloshing it all over. "And after that comment, I don't know if it will hurt the timeline or anything, but I believe I'm going to change the author of the books to Mary Elizabeth Leyton!" She turned back to help her mother.

"Nick, I wanted to thank you for the train." Rachel looked at him, and then at Ryan and John. "Nick bought Jamie a cute all-wooden train set!"

"All wooden except for the snaps," said Ryan. "Josiah told me."

"He never mentioned it to me," said Nick.

"He realized it wasn't worth the trouble." Ryan smiled.

"Who's Jamie?" Cora turned around and set the

58

heavy pot on the table. "Lamb stew! Eat up!"

John Mills took the serving spoon and heaped the stew onto his plate: chunks of lamb, carrots, celery, and potatoes. "Smells delicious, Cora!"

Cora sat down and looked at Rachel. "So, who's Jamie, Rachel?"

"Oh, sorry! The delicious stew broke my concentration. Jamie is a little boy whose grandparents left town for a few weeks. I'm taking care of him until they get back." She spooned stew into her plate. "Oh, this is amazing."

"Oh. Gone for a few weeks, huh?" asked John.

Nick saw him glance at his wife, and she had a frown on her face. Rachel, focused on the stew, didn't notice. "Yes, a few weeks," answered Nick. "Why?"

"John?" said Cora quietly.

John shrugged. "She should know, don't you think?"

Rachel swallowed and looked up. "Know what?"

"We saw this a lot when we lived in Atlanta. Granted, it may not be the same here, but often, people would ask friends to care for their children while they were away— only they never returned. I'm not saying that's going to happen with you, but you should be prepared that it's a possibility."

Rachel dropped her fork. "Oh." She put her head down. "You know, I had a feeling that was going to happen. His grandparents didn't tell him they were leaving, and they wouldn't even say good-bye to him. His grandfather said that it was better that way."

Cora shook her head. "Such a shame. If that happens, Rachel, what will you do with the boy?"

"Do with him? I'll keep him, of course. He has always been my favorite, and I already love the little guy."

"Usually the way it works," started John, "is that the house will come up for sale. When that happens, you know the people aren't planning to return. I haven't heard of any house coming up for sale, but tell me their last name, and I'll watch for you."

"The boy's last name is Givens. I'm not sure if they're his maternal or paternal grandparents."

"Oh, paternal. I know them. I didn't know they left town. Perhaps they *are* coming back," said John.

Nick looked at Rachel. Her silence spoke more than her words could. She was visibly upset. He felt immense compassion for her. Actually, he felt a lot more for her, and sitting across from her looking at her all night was not going to help. "How does adoption work in this century?"

"Adoption? There isn't any adoption. You want him? You keep him." John didn't even look up as he said it.

Nick reached across the table and patted Rachel's hand. "It will be all right, Rachel."

Ryan, quiet until now, said, "I heard a rumor today that the stagecoach is coming to town sooner than expected."

"Day after tomorrow," said John.

"That soon?" gulped Nick. "Shouldn't we do something? Have a big sign or something? What time are they coming?"

"Supposed to be here at one o'clock, but I wouldn't count on it," said John. "Stagecoaches are notoriously late."

Nick had one day to get a sign made. He liked celebrations, and the stage coming to town for the first time should be celebrated. The conversation went on around him, but he wasn't paying attention. Glancing up, he saw

Rachel looking at him. Although he couldn't make out the emotion in her eyes, he smiled at her. And when she smiled back and her eyes lit up, his decision was made. It didn't matter if she was a nineteenth-century girl or not. She lived in the nineteenth century, and that was good enough for him.

Dessert was delicious. Cora had baked a wonderful apple pie, and Ryan had brought in some ice cream from the cooler in his wagon. After everyone had moaned with delight and was dabbing at their mouths with a napkin, Rachel stood up.

"Thank you so much for supper and conversation, but I left Jamie with Josiah, and I told him that I'd be back soon. But I have time to help with the dishes."

"Oh, no," said Cora. "You are a guest. No dishes for you! Mary Elizabeth can help me."

"Sure, Mama. Ryan, can you take Rachel back home, please?" Mary Elizabeth stood up and grabbed a couple of plates.

"Not necessary," said Rachel. "It's not that far, and it's a beautiful night for a walk."

Nick stood up quickly. "I can escort you home, Rachel." He looked at Cora and John. "And thank you so much for supper. It was delicious!"

"Let's do it again, Nick! It's great to have another Mason around!" John held up his glass as if to toast Nick.

"After you, Rachel." Nick held out his arm in front of the door.

Nick told Rachel about his plans to get the sign, and before long, they were standing in front of her door. "Good night, Rachel." He leaned forward to give her a good-night kiss.

CHAPTER THIRTEEN

ALTHOUGH KISSING NICK was something that she thought she wanted, when she saw him coming toward her with his eyes closed and his lips puckered, she involuntarily stepped back and put her hand on his chest. "Good night, Nick." She turned toward her door, turned the handle, and was about to step inside. "Oh, tarnation!"

Nick, who had turned and taken a few steps away, quickly turned back. "Tarnation? You really are a nineteenth-century girl!"

That made her laugh. "No, I mean yes, but Jamie. I need to go get him." She stepped toward Nick.

"No worries, Rachel. I'll go get him and bring him home for you." He strode quickly away.

"Nick," she called after him. "Are you sure?"

"Positive. Be back soon."

Rachel walked inside the house, opened a drawer by the door, and fished out the two flickering flashlights that she had. She thought if they flickered, then they would more resemble a candle. Putting one on the table, she carried the other one out the back door and into the necessary. That thought made her laugh. Even *she* called the outhouse a necessary now. Walking back into the house, Rachel noticed that the flashlight on the table was gone, but there was light coming from Jamie's room.

When she walked in, Nick had just put Jamie on the bed, and was kissing him on the forehead. When Nick heard her, he turned around. "He was asleep when I got there. Do you want to put his pajamas on, or should I just cover him?"

Rachel smiled at Nick and looked at Jamie, lying there breathing softly. "Let's not disturb him. Just cover him. Thanks so much, Nick." He pulled the spread over Jamie and stepped back. Rachel put her hand on his arm. "Listen, Nick, about before."

Nick put a finger to her lips. "No, Rachel. That was my bad. Forget it. I'll see ya, soon. Good night." He walked past her out the door, and she could hear the front door close softly behind him.

She finished tucking Jamie in and then kissed him on the forehead. Taking the flashlight from his dresser, she flicked the switch and put it back in the drawer. The other one was still in her hand. Sighing deeply, she undressed and slipped into her own bed. Nick. She didn't know what to think about him. Yes, he was good looking and yes, he was good with Jamie. But was that enough? Then she let out with an "unh" that she thought might have woken Jamie. Shaking her head, she finally realized how wishy-washy she was. She liked Nick. She didn't like Nick. Couldn't she make up her mind? And with that confusion fresh on her mind, she fell asleep.

The following morning, she was awakened by Jamie once again jumping on her bed. "Wake up, Miss Jenkins! It's almost time for school! I had a good time with Josiah last night! Time for school! I didn't put my pajamas on last night!"

Rachel reached up and pulled him down beside her, snuggling. "Come here, you." She kissed his cheek. "I love you, you know that?"

"I love you, too, Miss Jenkins."

They arrived at school later than usual, but luckily she had all the supplies she needed for the day's lesson plans. The morning passed quickly, with Rachel giving special help for her remedial readers. When twelve o'clock came and all the children except Jamie were outside having dinner, she realized that she hadn't arranged for anyone to pick up Jamie's food. Standing up, she was heading toward the door to ask an older boy to walk up there, when Nick strolled in carrying Jamie's lunch.

"Delivery!" He handed it to Jamie, who hugged him and ran immediately out the door.

"Thank you, Nick. I appreciate that. How'd you get roped into that one? I thought you were going to go get the sign today?"

He nodded. "I am, but I still have time. I was over at the hotel doing some carpentry for Granny, and she asked if I would bring this over. Of course I said yes!"

"Thank you!"

Nick looked around the room. "There's no desks?"

"No, I keep meaning to find some and bring them back here, but—"

Nick stepped toward the door. "Hey, can I bring you back anything from—"

"Yeah, if you wouldn't mind—some easy reading books for Jamie. That would be awesome, Nick."

"Dare I bring back Dr. Seuss? Or do you think Ryan and Josiah would reprimand me?"

She chuckled and smiled at him. "Whatever you can find, Nick. And thank you so much for doing this for me."

"Doing it for you—and Jamie," said Nick, smiling.

Rachel nodded her head. "And Jamie. Thanks." She watched as he walked away from the school. When he got to the corner, he unexpectedly turned around and waved. Waving back, she stepped outside to find Jamie.

CHAPTER FOURTEEN

AFTER DROPPING OFF Jamie's lunch at the school, Nick hurried over to the livery. He asked Shiloh if he wanted to ride out today, and when Shiloh answered in the affirmative, Nick brushed and saddled him. Working in the morning at the hotel had delayed him, and now he'd have to hurry if he wanted to get everything finished in time—especially since he had even more to do now that he had stopped at the school.

Following the well-hidden trail that he and Ryan had finished, Shiloh kept wanting to veer over to the old trail. Nick had to explain to him there was a new trail now. When they arrived at the cave, Shiloh was more at ease. They arrived at the ranch house after a brisk canter down the main trail. Shiloh had been there so many times that he felt at home. And when Nick removed his bridle, filled the water, and threw a little hay into the feed bin, Shiloh barely nickered when he walked away.

Both Zack's and Madison's vehicles were gone, so Nick jumped into his truck and drove off. His first stop was the sign store. He would order the banner, put a rush on it, and hope they would finish by the time he had completed all his other errands. The man in the sign store charged him twenty-five extra dollars for expedited service, but Nick paid it gladly.

Next he stopped at the local college. He walked into the administration offices and asked about chair-desks. They often recycled their old ones when they got new ones. He lucked out. They had twelve left from their last giveaway. Nick took them all and loaded them into the back of his truck. That would be a great surprise for Rachel—though he would have to borrow Ryan's wagon to get them back to the old Red Bluff.

As he was driving to the humane society thrift store, he had to stop himself from pulling into the parking lot at Toys'R'Us. Although he would have loved to buy Jamie more toys, he told himself that it wasn't appropriate. So he continued driving. After pulling into the thrift store parking lot, he parked and walked in. They had a large book section, and he walked around until he found the children's books. First, he scoured the shelves for Dr. Seuss books. When he had gathered up all of those he could find—five of them all together including *The Cat in the Hat* and *The Cat in the Hat Comes Back*—he picked out a couple other books that he thought might interest Jamie. He paid for the books, unlocked his truck, jumped in, and drove to the hardware store.

It took him a while to find a rope that would be appropriate for the nineteenth century. He hadn't taken the time to look it up on the internet, but he imagined back then they made ropes from hemp. No chance of finding anything like that now. He picked out a cotton rope and bought two of them. At the cash register, though, they had packages of Tootsie Rolls, so he bought one of those, too. Jamie would like that. Then he returned to his truck. Now, all he needed was the banner.

As Nick drove back to the sign store, he sighed deeply, happy with himself. Everything he did today—except the sign—was for Rachel and Jamie. He didn't know whether Jamie was abandoned or not, but somehow he already thought of them as a team. A team that he wanted to be a member of. Nick shook his head to escape the thoughts he was thinking. What happened to the "I'm never getting married" Nick? He shrugged his shoulders. Believing that's what he wanted was comfortable for him —and right for him—*then. Now* thinking about being a family with Rachel and Jamie was comfortable and something that he wanted. Thinking back on the aborted kiss, he thought maybe that might not be what Rachel wanted—at least not yet. But he felt confident that he could change her mind. At least he felt sort of confident.

Pulling up into the parking lot for the sign store, Nick looked at the banner and smiled when he saw how perfect it was. He paid, put the banner in his truck, and drove back to Zack and Madison's house. Both vehicles were still gone, so he didn't bother to knock on the door. Instead, he moved all the chair-desks into his horse trailer that was parked at the front of the parking area, and covered them with a tarp.

Then he took the backpack that he kept there in case he forgot to bring one—which, in his haste, he had forgotten—and stuffed it with the books, Tootsie Rolls, and the rope. The banner wouldn't fit. It was much too big. So he rolled it up and decided that Shiloh would have to endure it over the saddle. Luckily, he had ridden Shiloh today. Cisco was a little more touchy. No one but Nick could ride him, and everything had to be normal and the same. Anything different could send ole Cisco crow-hopping and bucking. He didn't do it on purpose, and he was much better than when Nick first got him, but he was still a bit uppity at any change.

After locking the truck, Nick walked to the barn, carrying the backpack and the rolled-up banner. He put the backpack on, slipped the bridle onto Shiloh, showed him the banner, and swung up into the saddle bringing the banner with him. He draped it over the saddle right in front of him, and encouraged Shiloh out through the gates and onto the main trail. When he got back, he would ask Ryan to help him with the banner first thing in the morning. It would be perfect!

CHAPTER FIFTEEN

THE FOLLOWING MORNING, Rachel woke up before Jamie and began making his breakfast. It was something that she wasn't used to—she normally just had coffee for herself—but it was something she didn't mind at all. She loved that kid, and if it turned out that his grandparents abandoned him—yes, that's what it was, she thought—then she would adopt him, or keep him, in a heartbeat.

Jamie came out of his room rubbing his eyes. "Mornin', Miss Jenkins."

She stepped toward him, picked him up, and swung him around. "Good morning to you, sir!" She kissed him on the cheek and wondered if he could ever call her "Mom." If it came to pass that she did keep him, she hoped that he could. Then she wondered about being a single mom in the nineteenth century. For a second, an image of Nick popped into her mind, but she brushed it away. As small a town as the old Red Bluff was, she didn't think it would be a problem at all. And there would be no stigma to raising him alone, because every-one would know that he wasn't really hers. Alone. Alone with a young boy. The thought made her shiver. It didn't scare her, but she did think it would be nice to have a man around—teaching him about baseball or whatever men taught their sons in the nineteenth century. Someone who would be willing to get down on the ground with Jamie and play with him—like Nick did. She pushed the thought away again, put Jamie down, and gave him his breakfast.

After Rachel got both of them dressed, she and Jamie arrived at the school early. As she sat at her desk going over lesson plans for the day, Rachel realized that she needed more paper. Just like old times, she thought. "Jamie, let's walk over to the store. I need some paper."

"Okay, Miss Jenkins." He put his paper and pencil down, stood up, and held out his hand for her to grasp.

They walked up the street toward the store. When Rachel opened the door and they walked in, Bear ran out of the back room and straight into Jamie's arms.

"Bear!" he gasped. "It's good to see you, too!"

"When did you meet Bear?" asked Rachel.

"Sheriff Josiah and I came over to let Bear outside and to play with him! It was fun!" The dog had pushed Jamie over and was licking his face, while Jamie tried unsuccessfully to push him away.

"Hi, Rachel!" said Mary Elizabeth from behind the front counter.

"Hey, Mary Elizabeth. Guess what I need more of?"

"Paper," they both said in unison and laughed. Mary Elizabeth reached behind her, pulled out a ream of paper, and placed it on the counter.

"Have you heard anything from your father about—" Rachel motioned with her head toward Jamie.

"No. Maybe you'll get lucky, and they'll come back," Mary Elizabeth said in a soft voice.

71

Rachel shook her head, smiled at Jamie, and looked back at Mary Elizabeth. "Oh, no. I'll get lucky if they *don't*."

"Oh. I didn't realize you were that serious about—you know"—she lowered her voice even more—"keeping him."

"I was serious all right. Here's money for the paper. Do I owe you anything more or am I caught up?"

Mary Elizabeth pulled out a ledger, turned a few pages, and looked up. "No, looks like you're all caught up. Are you going to bring the kids into the street for the big event?" When Rachel tilted her head and blinked, Mary Elizabeth added, "You know, the first stagecoach to come into town!"

"Oh, I completely forgot. They're due at one o'clock, was it?" Rachel brought her hand to her head.

"Yes, one, but they might be late."

"That's right. *Notoriously* late, I believe your father said! Yes, I'll gather up the kids and bring them out to see the festivities. Bye, now, Mary Elizabeth. Thanks for reminding me."

"I think you would have been reminded, anyway."

"Why?"

"Look out the window. Ryan and Nick were planning all morning and walked next door right before you got here. I'm sure they're out there by now."

Rachel looked out the window and saw Nick on a ladder tying a rope attached to a banner onto the roof of the hotel. Ryan held the ladder with one hand and the rest of the banner with the other. "I see them! We better be getting back to school. Come on, Jamie! Good-bye, Mary Elizabeth!"

"Good-bye!"

"Good-bye, Bear," said Jamie as he took Rachel's hand.

They stepped out the door, and Nick was still stretched up tying the rope. Rachel stopped and looked at him. She raised her eyebrows and nodded. He certainly was good looking. As she stood there blatantly looking at him, she wished that she could make up her mind. Abruptly, he finished tying the knot and looked her way. He saw her looking at him, and he smiled. Embarrassed, she smiled back and continued walking down the street.

Nick climbed off the ladder and crossed the street to talk to them. Ryan followed him across, unrolling the banner. "Do you see what I bought? Isn't it awesome?"

Rachel read the sign. "Welcome First Stagecoach to Red Bluff!" And it had fireworks all over it. "It's beautiful, Nick. But fireworks? Would anybody know what they are?"

"*Everybody* would, Rachel," said Ryan. "Fireworks have been around forever!"

Nick motioned toward Ryan. "I checked first!"

"Good choice!" said Rachel.

"Hi, Deputy Nick!" said Jamie.

Nick reached down and picked up the boy. "How are you, young man? Are you learning a lot in school?"

"Yes, Deputy Nick. And I'm playing with my toys that you gave me. Thank you."

Nick kissed him on the forehead and put him down. "You are very welcome." Nick turned toward Rachel. "Are you bringing the kids out for the celebration?"

"Sure am. But I'm not sure what time to come. John said they'd be late."

"This is their first trip here. I can almost guarantee that they'll be on time. They'll want to make a grand entrance."

"Okay, I'll have the kids out here a little before one o'clock."

"I'll save a good spot for them, then." Nick smiled at her and his eyes sparkled.

"Thank you, Nick!" She had to pull herself forcefully away from his gaze. And still, she felt confused.

"Bye, Deputy Nick!" Jamie turned around and waved to him with his free hand.

"Bye, Jamie!"

CHAPTER SIXTEEN

NICK WASN'T SURE what time to go outside to ensure a good spot for the kids. He stood up, walked past Josiah sitting at his desk, and then approached the window. Looking out, he saw a few people milling around, but no one lining up along the street yet.

"It's too early to go outside." Josiah didn't even look up.

"Josiah, I want to make sure I get a good spot for the kids."

"You'll have the whole street to pick from. It's not that big of a deal, Nick."

"It is to *some* of us, Josiah." With his hands on his hips, Nick stared at him. "I didn't bother putting that sign up for nothing. It's a celebration!" Nick walked out the door.

There still weren't many people on the street, but Granny and Edward were in front of the hotel, and a couple of people stood in front of the bank. Sarah looked over the swinging doors of the saloon. Nick walked over there.

"Hey, Sarah."

"Hey, Nick. Love your sign!"

Nick smiled. "Thanks! I thought this should be a cele-bration!"

"Absolutely!" Sarah pushed open the doors and then turned and looked back into the saloon. "Matthew! Don't wait too long!"

"Sarah, I need to save some spots for the school kids Can you help?"

"Doesn't look like you need to push anybody away."

Nick chuckled. "Yeah, I know, but if people start lin-ing up, I need to save some spaces. Will you help?"

"Sure, Nick."

"See, look." Nick motioned his arm up and down the street. More people were in front of the bank, and Ezra from the livery had come around the corner followed by two other men. Then Nick noticed that Rachel had come out of the school with the kids all lined up. He smiled.

"What's *that* smile for?" Sarah turned around to look. "Oh! Rachel! Hmmmm."

"Shut up, Sarah!" Nick had known her for a long time, and telling her to shut up was completely appropri-ate. He walked past her toward where Rachel was bring-ing the kids. Raising his arms so she would see him, he shouted, "Over here, Rachel!" Rachel had ten kids with her. He noticed Jamie first, of course, and then saw Oscar, the little delinquent that he had caught close to the cave. When they got close enough, Nick said, "Hallo, Billy Bob. Where's your friend Bobby Bill today?"

"Sick!" the boy answered without even looking up.

"Hi, Nick. Thanks for doing this," said Rachel.

"Not much to be done. I thought there would be more people around than this." Nick helped line the kids up in front of the saloon in two rows, taller kids in the back, shorter kids in the front.

Rachel looked around. "Yeah. I'm surprised, too. Hi, Sarah."

"Hey, Rachel," said Sarah.

Ryan, Mary Elizabeth, and Josiah were headed their way. "See?" said Josiah. "I told you it wasn't a big deal."

Just then, several people on horses, and two wagons approached from the west. And more people and another wagon approached from the east.

"Golly gee whiz, Josiah," said Nick shrugging his shoulders, "guess you don't know the Old West."

"He's a flatlander," said Ryan.

They all laughed. "What's a flatlander?" asked Jamie.

Oscar, standing behind him, said, "Shut up, kid!" and shoved him.

Rachel grabbed Oscar by the arm and said, "Oscar! Don't you dare do that to him again! Or anybody! Just stand there and behave!"

"Or what?" sneered Oscar defiantly.

Nick stepped up to him. "Or I'll squash you like a bug!"

Oscar pretended he was shivering. "Oh, I'm scared, I'm scared," he said in a mocking high pitched voice.

"Are you okay, Jamie?" asked Rachel.

"I'm fine, Miss Jenkins."

All the people who had just come into town were milling around and lining up and down the street, with more coming all the time. The street was getting crowded. Nick glanced over at Josiah, raised his eyebrows, and smiled. Josiah shook his head and looked away. "Flatlander," whispered Nick, loud enough for Josiah to hear. Josiah laughed almost inaudibly, but didn't look at him.

Something moved at the edge of Nick's vision, and he

turned to look up the street. There was a man on horse-back galloping into town.

"The stagecoach is coming! The stagecoach is coming! Get ready!" He rode right on past them and around the corner. The next thing that Nick saw was the stagecoach coming with four beautiful,black horses cantering at the edge of town.

"They don't canter the whole way, do they?" asked Nick. "That seems cruel."

"It's just for show, Nick. Chill," said Josiah.

When they got to the corner, everyone started clapping. The horses were thirty feet away, when Nick heard Oscar say, "Here, you can see better from there!" And he pushed Jamie right into the horses' path. Nick pushed the kids aside, ran into the street, grabbed Jamie, and rolled out of the way of the horses just as they passed.

Most everyone had been so focused on the stagecoach that they didn't notice, but he had heard Rachel scream. Still shaking, he lay there in the dusty road with Jamie still in his arms. The stagecoach stopped just past them, and the crowd was all cheering and clapping.

"Deputy Nick?"

Nick was still trying to catch his ragged breath. "Yes, Jamie."

"Thank you for saving me. That was scary."

"You're welcome." Nick couldn't help it. As he hugged the boy tightly to him, tears came into his eyes. He was going to try to stop them from flowing, but he didn't have the strength.

Then Ryan ran over to him and said, "You okay, man?"

"Yeah, Ryan, I'm okay. And so is Jamie, aren't you,

little one?"

"I'm fine, Deputy Nick." Jamie looked at Ryan. "Deputy Nick saved me."

Ryan nodded at the boy. "I saw that!" Then he leaned over and extended his hand to help Nick up.

"Thanks, Ryan." Nick took his hand and pulled himself and Jamie up. Then he looked at the sidelines. Rachel was standing there, surrounded by the kids, and with a horrified expression on her face.

Nick walked over with Jamie and put a hand on Rachel's shoulder. "He's fine, Rachel. He's fine."

Jamie ran to her open arms and said, "I'm fine, Miss Jenkins. Deputy Nick saved me."

Rachel picked Jamie up with one arm, put the other arm around Nick, and pulled him close. She looked into his eyes and said, "Thank you, Nick." Then she gently placed her lips on his and kissed him.

CHAPTER SEVENTEEN

WHEN RACHEL LEANED back to look at Nick, he had a shocked but pleased look on his face. He smiled, and she smiled, and they stood there for a moment until Jamie said, "Can you put me down, please?" And that made them both laugh. Rachel put Jamie down, and he merged with the other students. Rachel looked at them.

"Where's Oscar?" Just then, she heard a blood-curdling scream coming from the jail and saw Josiah walking toward them. "What was that?"

"That, Rachel," said Josiah, with a satisfied look on his face, "was that little hoodlum student of yours who almost killed Jamie. I told him that he was under suspicion of attempted murder, and I locked him up. He didn't think I was going to lock the door and leave him there, so when I walked away and he heard the door close, he screamed. Or, as my lovely wife would put it"— he leaned closer to Nick and Rachel so only they could hear—"he freaked out."

"Jail! Oh, my!" Rachel frowned and shook her head. "He deserves it, though." She glanced at Jamie laughing with the other children. "That was so close. If Nick had been a second later—"

"They *both* would have been killed," said Josiah, soberly.

"And what would I have said to Jamie's grandparents?" Rachel shook her head.

No one heard anyone approach, so when John Mills spoke, it shocked them all. "No worry about that, I'm afraid." He held out a telegram to Rachel. "I received one, and you received one. Hope you don't mind me delivering."

"No. Thank you very much, John."

Before Rachel had removed her telegram from the envelope, John said, "I can guess what's in there. Mine said to please put their house up for sale, that they wouldn't be returning."

"Maybe Rachel's telegram will say to put the kid on the stage to wherever they are," said Josiah.

Rachel fished the telegram out of the envelope, opened it, and read it aloud. "We will not be returning. Please find a good home for our grandson." Rachel snorted. "Find a good home for our grandson? Like he's a puppy or something? And no 'thank you' for taking care of him or anything!" She exhaled sharply and turned toward Jamie.

"What are you going to do?" asked Josiah.

"Keep him, of course. I love the kid. It's just how they did it that infuriates me. They didn't even have the courtesy to say good-bye to him."

Nick put his arm around Rachel and squeezed her. "I'm not going to say 'I'm sorry' because I know you want this. But it's a big responsibility. So I *will* say that I will help out as much as you want me to."

"And I'll take care of him anytime you need me to,

81

Rachel. I think the kid is awesome, and I'm happy to do it anytime," said Josiah.

"Thank you, both of you," said Rachel. She didn't pull away from Nick, although she thought she should, in front of the whole town like that.

"Oh! That reminds me! I have the books you wanted!" Nick turned to walk away.

"No, wait!" Rachel called after him. "Not now. Will you come back to school with me? I'm still pretty shaken up."

Nick turned back and smiled. "Yes, of course." He put his arm around her, squeezed, and then let go.

"Thanks, Nick! Okay, boys and girls! The excitement's over! Let's go back to school now. There's not much time left. Line up."

All the students, and she and Nick, walked slowly back to school. Jamie jumped up and down and insisted on holding Nick's hand on the way back because Nick had saved him. Rachel grabbed Jamie's other hand, and the three of them walked down the street, with the other students in front of them. They left all the festivities behind.

When they walked into the classroom, the kids were still excited about the stagecoach and wouldn't settle down. Rachel felt weak and not able to control the class. She had not yet recovered from what happened with Jamie. She looked at Nick and raised her eyebrows. He looked at her hesitantly, and when she nodded her head, he stepped up to the front of the classroom.

"Okay, class, my name is Deputy Nick. Some of you may know me, and some don't, but now you all do." He smiled warmly at the class as they started to settle down.

"We know who you are! You're the one who saved

little Jamie from that scalawag Oscar!"

"We hope that Sheriff Josiah keeps him in jail, and when he gets out, makes him ride out of town on a rail!"

As Rachel listened, she realized how disliked he was by the other students. When she thought about it, his only friend was Reuben. She wondered what would have happened had Reuben been there today. Would he have defended Oscar? Could he after what happened?

A loud voice in the back of the room disturbed her thoughts. "Hey, you! I need to talk to you!"

Rachel turned around to see a heavyset man with a scowl on his face. He stood at the back door of the classroom with his hands on his hips. It was Oscar's father. She didn't like him addressing her as "hey, you," and she didn't like him bursting into her classroom with no courtesy at all. No wonder his son was such a scalawag, as the kids put it.

"I'm sorry, but we're in the middle of class now." Rachel looked at him, but stayed where she was and didn't move.

The man squinted his eyes and pointed at her. "I said I need to talk to you!" He stomped toward her.

From her peripheral vision, she saw that Nick had stiffened and turned toward her. Between Nick defending her and the man stalking her, she decided the best course of action would be to yield to the man. She couldn't have a confrontation happen in front of the children. As angry as the man looked, she hoped he wouldn't hit her, but if he did, she felt confident that Nick would come to her rescue.

She walked quietly toward the man and said, "Outside." He turned and stalked off through the door, and she heard Nick resume talking to the class. "How can I help you?"

He grunted. "I heard what happened. That my boy hurt the Givens boy."

Rachel nodded. "He pushed him in front of the running horses. Jamie could have been killed."

"It should have been Oscar gotten killed. It would serve the little no-account right." The man shifted on his feet, looked Rachel in the eyes, and squinted at her. "I also heard that he's in jail now."

"Yes, that's right. Josiah thought it would be a good lesson for the boy." Rachel, who had to push down the fear when she first stepped outside, now had worked her courage up. "Perhaps you should consider leaving him there overnight. That's something that he'll remember."

"Oh, no!" He tapped his heavy leather belt with a large metal buckle. "*This* will be his lesson tonight. I guarantee you that he won't forget it."

Rachel couldn't help but cringe. "Sir, you should consider leaving him in jail overnight instead."

The man stepped forward and poked Rachel in the chest with his forefinger. "*Nobody* tells me what I can do with my kids! Nobody tells me what to do with my girl, and nobody gonna tell me what to do with my boy!"

Rachel involuntarily stepped back. "You have a daughter, too? Why isn't she in school?" She didn't know what possessed her to speak up like that, but she did.

"She stays at home and does what I say to do! Girls have no reason to learn to read and write. Oscar don't either, but his mother insisted, thinking that it would calm him down. Obviously, she was wrong! I may have to reconsider! That's all I have to say!"

Without another word, he turned and stomped away from the school. He jumped into his wagon, whipped the horses, and took off up the street toward the jail. Rachel couldn't stand Oscar—especially after what he had done to Jamie—but right now, she felt sorry for him. She thought about the man's heavy leather belt and shivered.

CHAPTER EIGHTEEN

AFTER THE STUDENTS went home for the day, and Jamie once again jumped into Nick's arms to thank him for saving him, Rachel told Nick about Oscar's father. She had waited until Jamie was busy with his drawing again, so he wouldn't hear.

Nick shook his head. "What Oscar did was a terrible thing. I know that. He almost got Jamie *and* me killed. But a heavy belt? On a child? Unthinkable. It makes you wonder what came first—the mistreatment or the kid being a jerk."

"I know. I shudder when I think of that belt."

"There's nothing we can do about it. This is the nineteenth century. They beat children, and there are no child labor laws. There's nothing we can do."

Rachel nodded. "I know."

"Hey! I have an idea! Let me take you out to dinner tonight—I mean supper! What do you think? We'll go out to the hotel and live it up. Maybe Ryan has more ice cream put away, and we can get some!"

Rachel slowly shook her head and looked at Jamie. "Oh, no, Nick, I couldn't leave him. Not tonight. Not after what happened."

"No! I meant the three of us! I'll take both you and Jamie out to dinner! Come on! It will be fun!" The look on Rachel's face when he said he'd take them both out delighted Nick. It was a look of surprise and warmth, like it was the kindest thing anyone had ever done for her. And there was something else that he thought maybe was a threat of tears—because she kept blinking her eyes as she looked at him.

She walked over to where Jamie was drawing and kissed him on the top of the head. "We would love to come to supper with you, Nick."

Jamie looked up quickly. "We're going to eat supper with Deputy Nick? Are you coming to our house to eat, Deputy Nick?"

"No, buddy, I'm going to take you and Rachel—I mean Miss Jenkins—out to eat at the hotel. What do you think about that?"

"I've never gone out to eat before," Jamie said shyly.

Rachel smoothed her hand over his head. "You'll have a great time, Jamie. You'll love it."

Nick walked toward the door, and Rachel followed him. "How about if I pick you both up at five o'clock? Is that all right? Then I can bring the books over. Okay?"

She smiled warmly at him. "That's perfect, Nick. Thank you."

"No problem. My two"—he hesitated and looked down, then made a decision and looked her in the eye —"my two favorite people!" Then he walked out the door.

Rachel had wanted to ask him something else, but she was so stunned by what he had just said that she couldn't say a word. She could only stand at the door and watch him walk away. When he got to the corner, he turned around and waved, as she thought he would, and she waved back, smiling. It wasn't that she didn't *want* to be one of his favorite people, it was that the day had been so fraught with emotions—Jamie almost getting killed, and Nick saving him, and finding out that Jamie's grandparents weren't returning—that she didn't have room to be excited or maybe terrified that Nick considered *her* to be one of his favorite people. All she could feel right now was numb.

"Come on, Jamie. Let's go home." Performing simple duties by rote was all she could do, because there were no thoughts in her head. The rumbling sound of her emotions churning in the background made no room for them.

Two hours later, after a bath made from pans of heated water, she felt better. Jamie had gotten a bath, too. She thought that she could wash all the remnants of the day out of him. At least she hoped so. She never wanted to come face-to-face with his mortality again. That was the scariest moment she had ever experienced. And Nick—her knight in shining armor—had saved him. She exhaled gratefully and smiled.

Nick. She couldn't wait to see him. If there were any remaining doubts about him before, they had now disappeared.

CHAPTER NINETEEN

NICK HAD WALKED away from the school with a huge grin on his face and feeling like his feet didn't touch the ground. He would have jumped up and clicked his heels, except he had thought that Rachel might be watching. When he had reached the corner and turned around to wave at her, she smiled and waved back. Feeling lighter than air, he had strode quickly to the sheriff's office, past Josiah, and into his room.

"Hey, Nick. What's up with that giant smile on your face, huh? You walked by me like you didn't even see me. What's on your mind?"

"I have a date. That's all I'm going to say, Josiah." Nick wanted to get the books and candy ready for Jamie, and he wanted to pick out some better clothes to wear.

Josiah laughed. "Well, since there aren't that many single women in this town, my guess is that it would have to be the lovely Rachel. Right?"

"I'm taking her and Jamie to dinner at the hotel tonight. That okay with you?"

"Ah, a real family affair, huh?" Josiah raised his eyebrows at Nick.

"Family affair? *I'm* not the marrying kind, Josiah!" Nick stopped a minute to look at his clean cowboy shirts and to think about Rachel. Reluctantly, he said softly, but loud enough for Josiah to hear, "At least I wasn't—now I'm not so sure about myself."

Josiah roared with laughter. "Ah, the forever-single bad boy changing his ways. I never thought I'd see the day!" He stood up. "I'm going to the hotel now, getting my bride and my baby, and going home. Can you hold down the fort? You know, after dinner, *and all*." Josiah erupted in laughter again, and not waiting for an answer, slipped out the door.

His exuberance gone, Nick's shoulders slumped, and he put down the cowboy shirts in his hand. Sinking down on the bed, he sighed deeply. *Family?* He wasn't ready for a *family*. Yes, he liked Rachel and all, and liked Jamie, but *family?* Maybe he should make up some excuse and cancel dinner. No! He had wanted to offer to be there for Rachel when she told Jamie the terrible news. There was no way to guess how Jamie would react to it, and with Nick there, it might go a little smoother. At the very least, he could give Rachel some support when she explained everything to the boy. No, he couldn't cancel. Maybe he was a bad boy once upon a time, but he was a good man now, and he would do the right thing.

Nick stood up and chose the green plaid cowboy shirt. Josiah had initially objected to the cowboy shirts that had snaps on them, because they weren't around in the nineteenth century. And while everyone tried to respect Josiah's wishes about not *contaminating* the nineteenth century with twenty-first-century items, no one thought that snaps would hurt much, and even Josiah's wife, Jenna, wore them.

After he pulled out his green-colored jeans from the makeshift closet, he laid them on the bed next to the shirt. Then he walked into the office and sat down. Flipping through the stack of wanted posters, Nick always felt disappointed that he didn't see some famous outlaw there—even though he knew that Billy the Kid, the Younger Gang, and Jesse James didn't come onto the scene until later. Then he stood up and looked out the window. While Red Bluff was normally a quiet town, with the influx of people arrived from the stagecoach, many of them were wandering around town. Nick sat back down. After an hour of sitting and flipping through posters, looking out the window, and walking back and forth, he walked into the bedroom to change his clothes.

There was still some time left before he should leave to pick up Rachel and Jamie, but he was too restless to concentrate on anything. So he picked up the books that he had bought for Jamie, sat at the desk, and began leafing through them. They made him laugh, and he looked forward to sharing them with the boy. Somehow it gave him a warm glow inside, and he thought that yes, he would like to be a father someday. Someday. And that didn't necessarily mean that he would like to be a father to Jamie and husband to Rachel. Although he wasn't ruling that out as a possibility. But the thought of it still made him feel funny inside, like he was trapped—the ole ball and chain came to mind—and he laughed at the image. But it still bothered him.

He went back to reading the books, and a little while later, picked up the Tootsie Rolls and the books, put them in a bag, and strolled down the street toward Rachel's house. Although what Josiah said and then Nick's subsequent thoughts bothered him, it didn't dampen his excitement about seeing Rachel. That surprised him, and he decided that he would just go along with it and enjoy the evening.

When he knocked on her door, Jamie answered. "Hallo, Deputy Nick! Come inside. Miss Jenkins is in the necessary."

Nick walked in as Rachel approached from the back of the house. "Hi, Nick!"

"Hi, Rachel. You know, if you want, I could make you a composting toilet."

Her eyes got wide as she grew excited. "Really? You'd do that for me? Thanks, Nick! I would really appreciate that."

"What's a commosting toilet?" asked Jamie.

"Com-posting toilet," said Rachel. "You'll find out soon enough!"

"Commosting toilet!" yelled Jamie, who ran out of the room and plopped down on the floor in front of his barn full of animals.

"Rachel, this is for you." Nick handed her a picture of red roses in a fancy vase. "It's the closest I could get. I would have gone *there* to get some, but I didn't have time."

Rachel laughed. "At least I don't have to search frantically for a vase to put them in! They've already got one! And I don't have to remember to water them! Thank you, Nick. That was sweet of you. What's in the bag?" She pointed to the bag that was still in Nick's hand.

"The books. And some Tootsie Rolls!" He shrugged. "I couldn't help myself."

"Well, don't tell Jamie about the books or the candy," she whispered. "He'll be too excited to eat his dinner."

"Listen, Rachel, I was thinking," Nick whispered. "I

was wondering when you're going to tell him about his grandparents."

"I've been wondering about that myself. It's just—with all the scary excitement of the day—you know."

Nick nodded. "Do you want to tell him tonight, you know, with me as backup?" When she was silent, Nick quickly added, "I don't want to infringe on your parental responsibility in any way, I just want to help, that's all. If you don't want me there, just tell me."

Rachel put her hand on his arm. "Nick, that's so thoughtful. It would make it much easier for me to tell him if you were there. I don't know what I'm going to say—how I'm going to tell him that they're never coming back—but I know that with you there, it will be easier." She squeezed his arm. "Thank you for offering to help, Nick. I appreciate it."

"You ready to go?" When Rachel nodded, Nick called out, "Jamie! Let's go eat!"

Jamie ran into the room and grabbed Rachel's hand. When Jamie had his head turned away, Nick grabbed the Tootsie Rolls out of the bag and stuffed them in his pocket.

The three of them walked outside and continued up the street laughing, talking, and holding hands, with Jamie in the middle. It made Nick feel like a family man. And what surprised him was that he liked it.

CHAPTER TWENTY

As they walked up the street, Nick noticed there was no one else walking. He wondered where they all went, since the stage wasn't going to leave until the following day. When they walked into the hotel, Nick realized where they had all gone. The dining room was nearly full. It was a small dining room, though, so not surprising. Three couples sat at three different tables, and a man alone—probably the stage driver—sat alone at a fourth table. Although there were still two empty tables, Nick hadn't counted on so many people around. He had been thinking of a quiet dinner for the three of them. Turning to Rachel, he said, "Do you want to do this another time?"

"I don't mind the crowd, do you, Jamie?" She turned to the boy.

"I want to eat out!" said Jamie, a little too loudly so everyone in the restaurant turned to look at them.

"Then let's do it." Nick led them to the table that was farthest from anyone else—though not that far. Leaning over to Rachel to whisper in her ear as he held out the chair for her, he said, "I guess I'll have to sneak him the

Tootsie Rolls for dessert. I can't show them in this crowd."

Rachel shook her head in answer, and Nick picked Jamie up, swung him around, and then placed him in the chair that he had struggled to climb into. "There ya go, big fella."

"Thanks, Deputy Nick!"

They sat at the table looking around the crowded room. Neither of them had ever seen it like that before—and probably neither had Granny, thought Nick. Then he saw Mary Elizabeth come out of the kitchen and bring meals to a table. He elbowed Rachel. "Look!"

Rachel turned her head and blinked in surprise. "Mary Elizabeth! What's she doing here?"

Mary Elizabeth, who had heard Rachel's exclamation, walked over when she finished serving the couple. "Hey, Rachel, Nick! Nice to see you two here—together. Granny asked me to work because of the crowd. It's too much for her and Edward. She asked"—Mary Elizabeth pointed to the doorway to the kitchen—"oh, there she is now. Kat. She's helping, too."

Nick watched Rachel take a quick glance in the direction Mary Elizabeth had pointed and then quickly turned away. He knew why. So did Mary Elizabeth. The whole town probably knew, but he wouldn't talk to Rachel about it. None of his business. Period.

"I'll come back in a minute to take your order. It's so busy!" Mary Elizabeth hurried back to the kitchen.

A minute later, Nick saw Granny, with a look of exasperation on her face, glance in their direction. Her gaze passed from Rachel to Jamie and settled on Nick. "Nick! Come here! Now! I need you!"

Nick raised his eyebrows to Rachel, shrugged his

95

shoulders, and trotted into the kitchen where Granny had disappeared. Looking around, he spotted Granny and walked over to her.

"Can you cook?" Before he could even answer, she handed him a heavy metal spoon. "Here. Doesn't matter. Just don't let that burn. Stir when needed." And she raced away.

It smelled delicious. Inside a cast-iron frying pan, he stirred the green beans and onions. Well, he was definitely ordering this, he thought. He smiled when he thought of Rachel and Jamie in the other room waiting for him. His family. The thought pleased him even more than he might have realized. Nick stirred the pan periodically until five minutes later when Granny took the spoon away from him without ceremony and said, "Thank you, Nick. You're a good boy."

As Nick walked out, he noticed Edward, Granny's husband, taking something out of the oven, and Kat and Mary Elizabeth rushing in and then out again carrying plates. There were three pies on the counter as he went through the doorway, and at least one of them was apple. Mmmmmm. He would have liked to have apple pie a la mode, but with all the people there, he couldn't risk it. Ah well, another time. Or maybe sometime he could take Rachel and Jamie to the new Red Bluff for dinner at a restaurant that served pie a la mode. That would be great! And then he remembered that Jamie didn't know about the new Red Bluff, and it probably wouldn't be a great idea to take him there. He was sure that Rachel wouldn't approve of that.

When he approached the table, he saw that Rachel had changed the way she was sitting. She was now sitting so she couldn't see into the dining room, and he knew that was to avoid Kat. Jamie sat there quietly beside her. What a great kid he was.

Smiling, Nick sat down and joined them. "Granny just wanted me to stir something."

Before Rachel could reply, Mary Elizabeth plopped down in the empty seat at their table. "Phew! This has been the busiest hour ever! I'm beat!" She briefly looked around the room at the tables and then pulled out her paper and pencil. "What can I get y'all? The special tonight is steak and a baked potato, and I would highly recommend it."

"Steak it is," said Nick. "Rachel, how 'bout you? Do you want steak, too?"

"Sounds great. What about Jamie?"

"I'll have snake, too. Is it rattler? I never had any, but my grammy said it tastes like chicken!"

They all laughed. "It's steak, Jamie, not snake." Turning to Rachel, Mary Elizabeth said, "I'll have them prepare a small portion for him." Then in a low voice, she said, "They haven't invented children's portions yet!" Standing up, she smiled and walked away.

"Wait! I was just stirring some green beans and onions in the back. Can we have some of that, too?"

Mary Elizabeth nodded. "Comes with it." And she disappeared into the kitchen.

"I've never seen it so busy in here." Nick looked around the room.

"It's never *been* so busy in here! The stagecoach coming to town is going to change everything." Rachel looked at Nick and then smiled at Jamie. "How is your first dining experience, young man?"

"I'm hungry!"

"The food will be here soon, Jamie. They still have to

cook it." Rachel stroked his head.

"Does Deputy Nick have to help?"

Nick laughed. "No, that was a special circumstance, Jamie. Granny and Edward got so busy that they couldn't handle it alone. I think they have it under control now."

"I'm glad. I like it when you're here with me and Miss Jenkins."

Rachel looked at Nick and raised her eyebrows. He knew she was asking if they should tell him now, so he shook his head. "Let's eat first."

CHAPTER TWENTY-ONE

WHILE THEY WERE waiting for their dinner, Nick suggested playing an alphabet game with Jamie. They went through the alphabet one letter at a time, and each person had to think of an item that began with that letter. Nick and Jamie both did really well, but with Kat in the room, Rachel was distracted. They had gotten up to "S" when dinner came. Rachel smiled when she saw that Mary Elizabeth had already cut Jamie's steak into really small pieces. "Thank you, Mary Elizabeth."

"No problem! Enjoy your supper!"

Jamie dug into his steak and potato. He left the green beans and onions alone, until Nick made exaggerated moans of delight when he ate them. Without saying a word, Jamie tried one, tried another, nodded his head, and finished them along with the steak and potato.

When they had all finished eating, Nick put his hand in his pocket, and then she heard him fiddle with a wrapper under the table. He turned to Jamie and whispered, "Do you trust me?"

Jamie nodded his head vigorously. "You're Deputy Nick, and you saved me!"

"Okay, little man. I'm going to put something in your hand. You can't show it to anybody, and you can't look at it. Just put it in your mouth, and I guarantee that you'll like it. Can you do that?"

"Yes." Jamie stuck out his little hand in front of Nick.

Nick dropped something in his hand, closed it, and pushed it back to Jamie. "Go ahead. Eat it."

Jamie opened his hand without looking and stuck the item into his mouth. His eyes lit up as he chewed, and he put his hand back out to Nick. "More, please!"

Nick laughed and put another in his hand. Jamie stuck it in his mouth, smiling happily.

"What is it?" asked Rachel.

Nick motioned with his head, and Rachel held out her hand to him. Nick filled it and nodded. She stuck it in her mouth and discovered the delightful chocolatey taste of the Tootsie Roll. She burst out laughing.

"More, please." Jamie stuck his hand out to Nick again.

"More, please." Rachel stuck her hand out to Nick.

They all laughed, and Nick stuck one in his mouth. "Mmmmm mmmmm good!"

"More, please," said Jamie.

"I think you've had enough sugar for one night, young man." Rachel pushed his hand down.

"Please, Deputy Nick?" asked Jamie, looking up at Nick with his big, brown eyes.

"Isn't he the charmer?" asked Rachel.

"I'm sorry, Jamie, but Rachel says no. Sorry. There will be more later."

"Okay." Jamie frowned and looked down at his hands.

"This probably isn't the best time, huh?" Rachel glanced at Nick.

"Oh, sorry. We probably should have before I gave him the candy."

"Let's play the alphabet game again," said Jamie.

"I think we've had enough of that." Rachel put her napkin on the table.

"Let's go play with my ball! Or the train! Or the farm!"

"I think somebody has had too much sugar. Sorry, Rachel." Nick looked at her sheepishly.

"No, it's fine, Nick. How about if we walk around town and use up some of his energy?"

"Sounds perfect." Nick stood up, reached into his pocket, and put a dollar bill on the table.

Mary Elizabeth, who was walking by, grabbed it up, stuck it in her pocket, looked around, and whispered, "Nick!"

"Oops, sorry. I wasn't thinking!"

"You can pay tomorrow," said Mary Elizabeth. "Now skedaddle before you contaminate the time line!"

Nick and Rachel laughed and walked toward the door. Jamie ran around the restaurant and, without looking up, ran right into Granny coming out of the kitchen.

"Tarnation, child! What's gotten into you? I thought you were a quiet little boy."

"Sugar's gotten into him, Granny. Sorry."

"Sugar! Sugar! Sugar!" Jamie started jumping up and down until Nick picked him up and carried him out the door, followed by Rachel.

She was grateful that she could leave the restaurant without having to face Kat. Now she stepped outside and breathed the fresh air, while Nick spun Jamie around, with Jamie squealing with delight. Nick put him down.

"Hey, pardner. How about if I race you to the

corner?"

"Yeah," Jamie said before racing off in front of Nick.

"Hey, that's not fair!" Nick ran after Jamie, easily catching up. As he ran past him, he picked him up again and carried him to the corner.

Rachel followed them, enjoying how well they got along. Nick was quite the man, thought Rachel. But now her thoughts turned to Jamie. They had to tell him. Sugar or no, it had to be done. When they raced past her going the other direction, Rachel nodded toward Nick, and he slowed down.

"Hey, Jamie, come 'ere."

"Okay, Deputy Nick." Jamie ran up to Nick and jumped into his arms.

Nick, caught unawares, stepped backwards. "Whoa, pardner. Time to calm down. Can you do that?"

Jamie nodded his head. "I think so, Deputy Nick."

"Let's walk home, shall we?" Rachel started walking toward her house.

Nick put Jamie down and grabbed his hand before he could run off again. Rachel took Jamie's other hand. They walked down and across the street and approached her house. She looked at Nick and said quietly, "Let's get him settled down first."

Nick nodded and opened the door for them to enter.

CHAPTER TWENTY-TWO

THE THREE OF them sat on the floor. Rachel sat behind Jamie, stroking his head, while Nick sat in front of him as they played with the wooden train set. "Choo choo! Choo choo!" shouted Jamie. After twenty minutes of pushing the trains so hard down the tracks that they derailed every time, Jamie began to tire. When Rachel saw Jamie yawning, she nodded to Nick.

"Let's go in the other room, okay, buddy?"

"Okay, Deputy Nick. I'm getting tired." He yawned again.

Nick picked him up, carried him into the living room, and put him on the big easy chair. Then he and Rachel kneeled in front of him.

Rachel took his hand. "Jamie, we have something to tell you. Something bad."

He yawned and blinked. "Okay."

"Your Grammy and Grampie aren't coming back." Rachel looked at him, and he didn't even flinch.

"Am I going to a orfage then?"

"Orfage?" Nick was confused.

"Do you mean orphanage, Jamie?" asked Rachel.

He nodded. "Unh huh."

"Who told you *that*?" Nick felt himself getting angry at whoever would tell the boy something like that.

"Oscar. He said that my grandparents weren't coming back, and I would have to go to a orphange."

Rachel patted his hand and noticed tears coming into his eyes. "I was thinking maybe you could stay with me. Would you like that?"

Jamie's eyes opened wide. "You mean you'd be like my mama?" When Rachel nodded, Jamie continued. "Would it be all right if I called you Mama?"

Rachel nodded. "Yes, that would be fine, Jamie." Her voice had inadvertently become higher, so Nick stole a glance at her. When he realized that tears were coming into her eyes, too, he put his arm around her and squeezed her close to him.

"Then can I call you Papa?" Jamie looked at Nick, his eyes full of hope.

Nick reached out and patted his shoulder. "Sorry bud, no. But you can call me just Nick."

"Just Nick?" Jamie asked.

"Yes, buddy. You don't have to call me *Deputy* Nick, anymore. Just Nick."

"Just Nick," said Jamie. "Then that's your first name?"

"Yeah, Nick."

"I mean 'Just.'" Jamie looked at him with a straight face.

Nick and Rachel were both confused. "Just? What do you mean, Jamie?"

"You told me to call you Just Nick, so I wondered if Just was your first name." A slight smile started spreading across his face.

"Why you little—!" Nick ruffled his hair. "Now you've

got a sense of humor, huh?"

Jamie yawned. "Mama? Can I go play with my trains some more?"

"Jamie, I think it's time for you to go to sleep."

"Okay, Mama." Jamie reached out his arms to Rachel. She stood up, wrapped her arms around him, and picked him up. Nick followed them into Jamie's room and helped Rachel get him undressed and under the covers. When Rachel bent down to kiss Jamie's cheek, he said, "I love you, Mama."

"I love you, too, Jamie."

Then Nick bent down to kiss him. Jamie surprised him by saying, "I love you, too, Just Nick." Then he chuckled, turned over, closed his eyes, and fell asleep.

As Rachel walked out the door in front of Nick, she turned her head and said, "Sugar crash."

"Well, he took it well." Nick followed her into the living room, and when she sat on the couch, he sat across from her.

"Yes, but that little jerk, Oscar. I could wring his neck."

"I was angry, too, when Jamie said that somebody told him that—until I found out it was another kid." Nick shrugged his shoulders.

"How do you think that Oscar knew Jamie's grandparents weren't coming back? *We* didn't even know until today."

"Probably heard his parents or someone else talking. You heard what John and Cora said—it happens all the time."

"Well, it's over with now. I don't have to worry anymore about what might happen *if* they don't come back. They're not coming back, Jamie is now mine, and all is well."

Nick nodded and pointed to her. "And now *you* have a lot of responsibility that you didn't have before. Are you okay with that?"

Rachel smiled and tilted her head. "I love him very much. There was never any doubt about that. And what you do for love is so much easier than anything that you *have* to do. I mean, cooking dinner every night will be a pain, but it's for someone I love, so it's okay."

"That's a good way to look at it, Rachel. And I'm happy to help all that I can." He reached across and took her hand. "I mean that, Rachel. I'd love to help." He almost winced when he realized that he had used the word love, but he consciously didn't pull his hand away.

She patted his hand. "Thank you, Nick. I really appreciate that. I do."

Then he leaned over and kissed her on the lips. When she didn't resist, he kissed her again, longer. Then he stood up, said good-bye, and walked out the door, still with the taste of her on his lips.

CHAPTER TWENTY-THREE

Rachel woke, stretched, and smiled. She had done the horrible deed—telling Jamie about his grandparents —and it had come out all right. He even wanted to call her Mama! Where was he? Usually, he would already be up and jumping on her bed by now. Maybe he was just tired from all the activity the night before. Sighing deeply, she turned over to look at the clock. She still had time.

It was then that she heard the sound. A low moaning sound. What was that? Then it occurred to her that it might be Jamie. Jumping up, she ran into his room and found him with a tear-streaked face.

"Mama. I hurt. I hurts bad, Mama."

"Where Jamie? What hurts?"

"My toof."

"Toof? What's a toof?"

When Jamie pointed to his mouth, she understood. Maybe he was losing a tooth. She asked him which one, and when he pointed to a lower front tooth, she gently put her finger on it to see if it was loose. It wasn't. A chill went through her. Oh, no! She shouldn't have let Nick give him all that candy! Now what was she going to do? There was only one thing to do in the nineteenth century —take him to the doctor. She scooped him up from the bed and was halfway to the front door, when Jamie said, "Mama, you're still in your nightgown."

"Oh, Jamie! You're right!" She laid him gently back on his bed. "I'll be back in a flash!" Then she raced into her room, stripped her nightgown off, and threw on one of her long dresses. It struck her as she was putting on her shoes. Kat. Kat and Doc were married now, and Kat would be there.

The thought of it brought the whole ugly episode back to her—the whole reason that she had avoided Kat the night before. Doc used to be a good friend of hers. She had walked over there every morning, and they would have coffee together. He had been her best friend. Once Jenna married Josiah and Sarah married Matthew, she didn't see *them* that often, and Doc's house was across from hers. Their friendship had grown over the months, and he was comfortable and fun. And although she had never felt any kind of *romantic spark* with him, she thoroughly enjoyed their time together. What possessed her that day to try to kiss him, she still didn't know. But unbeknownst to her, he and Kat had already gotten involved. And unfortunately, Kat walked in just as she kissed him, which almost ruined things between the two of them. Since then, she hadn't been able to face Kat, and hadn't had to—even living across the street from her. Somehow she had always managed to avoid it. But not now. To see Doc, she had to see Kat, too.

Pushing the thoughts from her head, she knew there was no way to avoid this meeting. Returning to Jamie's room, she found him struggling to get his shirt on.

"I got dressed, too."

Rachel helped him with his shirt, and when she bent over to pick him up, he said, "I can walk, Mama. It's just my toof."

"Okay, Jamie, let's go see the doctor."

She took his hand, held her head up, and walked across the street. The door to the doctor's office—which was also his house—was always open. She opened the door, stepped in, and said, "Is anybody up yet?"

Doc walked out from the kitchen. "Rachel! How good to see you! Who's this?"

Apparently Doc didn't hold any grudges against her. "This is Jamie."

"My toof hurts." Jamie pointed to his mouth.

"Come here, young man." Doc picked the boy up, carried him into the examining room, and put him on the table. "Open up."

Just then, Kat came downstairs and walked in. "Rachel," she said in a flat tone.

"Hallo, Kat," said Rachel.

"What is it, David?" Kat stood beside Doc.

"Look." Doc pointed at the boy's mouth.

"He had all this candy last night, but I didn't think it would do *this*. I feel so guilty," Rachel said quietly.

"Nothing to do with it, Rachel. Look here." While Doc pulled Jamie's lower lip away, Kat pointed at his mouth. "See. His permanent lower incisor is coming in, but his baby tooth isn't coming out. It needs to be pulled."

"Can you do it, Doc?"

Doc said, "Yes" at the same time Kat said, "He can do it, but he shouldn't. You need to take him to a regular dentist. That would be best for the boy."

109

"I agree," said Doc, standing back. "It's a simple procedure, but it should be done by someone more knowledgable than I about teeth."

"Who's boy is he?" asked Kat.

"I'm *her* boy. She's my Mama," said Jamie.

Rachel nodded. "He's mine, and I want to do what's best for him. But I have to teach school today." She bit her nails.

Just then, Nick burst through the door. "Is Jamie all right?"

"It's just his tooth. How did you know?"

Nick stepped up to Jamie and put his hand on the boy's cheek. "John stopped by and said he saw you coming in here."

"I'm fime, Just Nick," said Jamie, which made Rachel and Nick both laugh.

"Still have your sense of humor, huh, kid?" Nick smiled at the boy.

Jamie nodded. "My toof still hurts, though."

"Hallo, Nick," said Kat. "The boy needs to go to a dentist."

Nick looked at Rachel, who gave him a pleading look. "You have to teach, right?" Rachel nodded her head. "Do you want me to take him?"

Tears came into Rachel's eyes. "Could you?"

Nick put his arm around her and gave her a squeeze. "Of course. I told you I'd help out as much as I could. But what about—you know—the *new* Red Bluff?"

"It needs to be done, Nick." Doc put his hand on the boy's head. "I could do it, but it wouldn't be the same."

"Looks like you and me are going to take a little trip, pardner," Nick said to Jamie.

CHAPTER TWENTY-FOUR

THEY WALKED DOWN the street together, with Nick's arm around Jamie. Before they had left Doc's office, Kat had put some teething powder on Jamie's gums and had given the rest of the container to Nick in case they couldn't get an appointment right away. Nick didn't know what he was going to tell Jamie about the future they were about to visit, but he knew he'd have to talk to him about it before they arrived. Probably even before then—if they saw a plane on the way to the ranch, what would Jamie think?

As they walked into the livery, Jamie looked up at Nick. "But I don't know how to ride a horse."

"I know. You told me that, buddy. All you have to do is hold on to me. We'll ride double, so you don't have to know how to ride."

"But I want to."

"Want to what?"

"Want to ride."

"You'll ride with me." By this time they had arrived at the stall with Shiloh and Cisco, and the horses nickered when they saw Nick.

"What was that?" Jamie took a step backwards.

"That's called a nicker. It means they're glad to see you." Nick stroked both horses on the nose. "Do you want to touch them?"

Jamie hung back, unsure. "Will they hurt me?"

Before Nick could answer, Jamie said, "Okay," and stepped forward to touch both horses.

"I didn't say anything," said Nick.

"They did," said Jamie without looking at him. "They both said that they wouldn't hurt me."

"Oh. Okay." Nick felt a little hurt. He thought his horses only talked to him. Then he realized that if he had to choose someone else whom his horses talked to, Jamie would be his first choice.

"They say that they like me, and I don't have to be afraid." Jamie continued stroking the horses.

"Those horses talk to you, huh, little guy? Hey, Nick. Who's your friend here?" Ezra shook Nick's hand, handed him two brushes, and looked at Jamie.

"This is Jamie. He's Rachel's, er, son. Now. Jamie, this is Ezra."

"Hi, Ezra." Jamie turned, shook Ezra's hand when it was offered, and then turned back to the horses.

"Hallo, little one. Going for a ride today?"

"I'm riding with Nick. I don't know how to ride a horse yet."

"Well, I'm sure Nick will teach you, and I know he'll be a good teacher." Ezra looked at Nick. "Who're you riding? Shiloh?"

"Yep." Nick nodded.

"I'll get your saddle for you."

"Thanks, Ezra." When the man had walked away, Nick bent down to whisper in Jamie's ear. "Jamie, let's keep the talking to horses to ourselves, okay? Not everybody can do that."

"They can't? Really? Why not?"

"We'll talk about it later. Let me brush Shiloh, because we need to get going."

Nick walked into the stall, leaving Jamie outside. Then he brushed Shiloh until Ezra brought the saddle and saddle pad and placed them on the stall door.

"Been nice meeting you, Jamie. Hope you have a good ride."

"Thank you. We will."

Ezra laughed and walked away. When Ezra was almost out of sight, Jamie whispered loudly, "Why do I have to keep the talking to horses a secret, Nick?"

"Shhh. We'll talk about it later."

Nick walked Shiloh out of the stall, tightened the cinch again, and picked Jamie up and put him on the top rail of the fence. Then he swung up on the big paint and asked him to side-pass to the fence where Jamie was. "Come on, Jamie. Climb up behind me and put your arms around me."

"Okay, Nick."

After Jamie was securely in place, Nick asked, "You feel safe now?"

"Yes, Nick. Let's go."

They rode out of the livery and down the street, heading out of town. Turning off at the newly made hidden trail, they approached the cave. It had to be now.

"Jamie?"

"Yes, Nick."

"I need to talk to you about something important. Have you ever been in a cave before?" The horse walked slowly into the cave.

"No, Nick."

"Remember I told you not to mention talking to horses?"

"Yes, but I don't know why."

"I told you. Not everybody can do it. You're very special *and* lucky to be able to hear horses."

"Can you?"

"Yes, but nobody else I know—besides you—can."

"Oh."

"So you need to keep that a secret. You and I can talk about it between ourselves when we're alone, okay?"

"Okay. Shiloh says he wants to move through the cave."

Nick had stopped the horse in the middle of the cave to talk to Jamie, and now Shiloh was getting impatient. "I know! He told me, too. But the other thing that I have to tell you is there is another secret that I want you to keep. Can you do that? This one is even more important than talking to horses. Can I count on you?"

"Sure, Nick. What's the secret?"

Nick cleared his throat, not knowing exactly where to begin. "Well, just like not everybody can talk to horses, not everybody knows how to get to the place we're going."

"Can't somebody just show them?"

"Um, yes, but those of us who know how to get there don't want anybody else to know. Because, you know, it's a *secret*. It wouldn't be right for everybody to know. It's a special place, and not everybody would understand. It's also a strange place, stranger than anything you've ever seen before. And, it's a cool place! I know you'll like it! But you can't tell anybody that you've been there. You can't talk about what you've seen or what you've done.

114

Nobody. Do you understand?"

"Nobody? What about Mama?"

"Okay, here's the deal, Jamie. If Mama talks to you about it, she will be sure to do it when nobody else is around. So if *she* talks to you about it, then it's okay. Same with me. Understand?"

"Yes, Nick, I promise."

"Okay, there's more. Some of the new and strange things that are there might scare you. There are big machines that fly through the sky."

Jamie squeezed Nick's waist and giggled. "Now you're trying to hornswoggle me, Nick."

Nick tried to turn around in the saddle to look at Jamie, but could only catch a glimpse. "No, Jamie, I'm not. Maybe we'll see one on the way there." He urged the horse forward. "C'mon, Shiloh."

CHAPTER TWENTY-FIVE

THEY WERE THROUGH the cave and halfway to the ranch house when a plane flew overhead. First they heard it, and Jamie tightened his grip around Nick's waist.

"Look up, Jamie. It should be coming our way."

"You weren't kidding me, then?"

"No, Jamie. There it is now, look!" Nick felt Jamie shift behind him.

"Wow! Wow!" Jamie turned to watch the plane until it was out of sight. "I want to see another one!"

Nick laughed. "Nothing I can do about that, pardner. They only fly by when they fly by. We're almost there now." Nick leaned down, unlatched the gate, rode through it, and re-latched it. After going through another gate, they rode into the barn.

Nick leaned over and helped Jamie off the horse. Then he dismounted, led Shiloh into a stall, and checked to make sure there was plenty of water.

"I like riding, Nick. When can I ride my own horse?" Jamie looked up at him, hopefully.

"Well, pardner, we'll have to see what your mama has to say about that. Come on, let's go." Nick took Jamie's hand and walked toward the ranch house. He hoped that someone was home. Madison's car was there, but sometimes she rode in with Zack. Although the doors were always left unlocked, Nick didn't feel comfortable barging in like that. And he needed to use their phone to make an appointment with a dentist. Before that, he had to *find* a children's dentist.

When no one answered the door, Nick had a feeling that he should enter, although he didn't feel comfortable. Turning the handle, he tentatively stepped inside and said, "Hello! Anybody home?"

"Yeah," said a soft voice from the back bedroom.

"Madison? It's Nick."

"And Jamie!"

"I'm sick, Nick. Come on back."

In a way, Nick was grateful that Madison was sick. Usually she was rude to him because years before, her mother, Kat, had liked him. Nick would have thought that Madison was over it by now, since Kat was happily married to Doc in the nineteenth century. Walking into the bedroom, Nick saw that Madison looked pale and was all bundled up under the covers. "Oh, Madison, you look awful. Are you all right?"

"You always know what to say to a girl, Nick." She coughed out a laugh. "I'm taking aspirin, and I should be fine in a day or two."

"Can I get you anything?"

"If you could buy me some more orange juice, it would be awesome. Who's that?"

"I'm Jamie!"

"Madison, this is Jamie. Jamie, this is Madison. You know the nice woman at the doctor's office, Kat? That's Madison's mother."

"Oh. She was pretty. She said I need a dentist, but I don't know what that is," he explained.

"So that's why you're here. Who is he, though?" Madison coughed again.

"He's Rachel's son."

"Rachel? I didn't know she had a son. But he looks like he's from—*there*. Is he adopted?"

"I'm dopted. Rachel is my mama now."

"Ah, I see." She looked at Nick. "He's cute as a button, Nick. But you oughta get him some decent clothes before you go out in public."

Nick looked down at the boy, noticing his clothes for the first time. He had on a loose shirt buttoned down the front and connected with buttons to the top of his pants. His loose pants had buttons on the side. His shoes were boot-like and also had buttons.

"And get him some sneakers, too, while you're at it." She coughed.

"What are sneakers, and why do I need them?" asked Jamie.

"They'll make you look cool, kid!" Madison turned over in her bed. "I'm done, Nick. The phone is in the living room, and if you need a computer, there's one in Jenna's old room just down the hall and to the left. Good luck at the dentist, Jamie!"

"Thank you, Madison." Jamie followed Nick out of the bedroom.

Madison sounded so horrible that Nick didn't want to bother her to find out where a phone book was, so he turned on the computer in Jenna's bedroom. "See this, Jamie? It's called a computer. It does all kinds of cool things. Today, we're going to look up where to take you to the dentist. Oh! How is your tooth? Is it still hurting?"

118

"A little." Jamie put his hand on the front of his pants. "I have to use the necessary, Nick. Where is it?"

"Down the hall to the left." Nick stared at the computer screen waiting for it to be ready.

"Better show him how to do it, Nick," coughed Madison from the bedroom.

"Oh, yeah." Nick walked with Jamie down the hallway and turned into the bathroom. He turned on the light and pulled Jamie in with him.

"What's this?" Jamie looked around the room not understanding.

"Remember I told you there were some strange things here—you know—like the plane?"

"Yes, but I need a necessary."

"Let's put more of the teething powder on your sore tooth, first. It will just take a minute." After applying the powder, Nick explained how to use the toilet and how to flush, and then he left Jamie alone in the room. As he was walking out, he turned back and said, "When you're finished, wash your hands at the sink, over there." He pointed to the sink and walked back to the room with the computer.

Five minutes later, Nick had a list of children's dentists in front of him on the screen, and at the same time, he realized that Jamie was still in the bathroom. When he heard the toilet flush, he called out, "Jamie? What are you doing in there?"

"Pressing this handle and watching the water go down! It's some pumpkins!"

"Jamie, wash your hands and come in here." Nick wrote down the dentists' telephone numbers.

"Okay, Nick."

As Nick walked toward the living room where the

phone was, Jamie came out of the bathroom smiling. "I like this place, Nick! Can we stay here? Mama, too?"

Nick smiled and put his arm around Jamie. "Sorry, buddy, we all live in another place, and that's where we're going to stay. Come on, I'll show you something else that's cool." In the living room, he picked up the telephone and showed it to Jamie. "I can talk to people on this. People from far away."

"Can you talk to Mama?" Jamie jumped up and down. "I want to talk to Mama!"

"She's a little too far away, Jamie, sorry. But I have to find you a dentist now."

After five calls including a couple of dead ends, Nick found a dentist and secured an appointment at 10:00. "Well, we have some time before your appointment. Shall we go get you some different clothes?"

"Nick! Nick!" called Madison softly from the bedroom.

"Yeah, Madison?" Nick walked into the hall to hear her better.

"I just thought of something. There's a carnival in town. I think the rides start at eleven or twelve o'clock. Jamie might like that."

"Thanks, Madison! We're going to get him some clothes now, and we'll check out the carnival after his appointment, if he's up to it. Hope you feel better."

CHAPTER TWENTY-SIX

RACHEL WAS SO relieved that Nick volunteered to take Jamie to the dentist. There was no way she could get away. It wasn't like the twenty-first century where she could call all the parents and call off school. And if it wasn't called off, who could she have asked to substitute for her? Mary Elizabeth? Possibly, but most likely, with the stagecoach still in town, Mary Elizabeth would be at the hotel helping Granny. There was no one else she could ask. And though Nick probably would have volunteered to do that, too, *she* was the teacher, and she took her job seriously. Not that she didn't take parenting seriously—she did. But it was all so new to her and a little overwhelming. Okay, if she was honest with herself, it was a lot overwhelming. And there was Nick, ready to help out as soon as she needed him.

Nick. Tears almost came to her eyes when she thought about how wonderful he was to do this for her and for Jamie. What a great man! She sighed. He was always there when she needed him. He was always there for her. Who else in her life had been like that? Yes, she had friends, but this was different. And yes, there had been men in her life before, but none who treated her as well as Nick treated her. None whom she could count on like she counted on Nick. He was wonderful, and she was falling in love with him.

The thought caught her so much off guard that she gasped, which made her cover her mouth and giggle. She was in love! How long had it been since she was in love with anyone—had allowed herself to be in love with anyone? A year or two or maybe three before she moved to the old Red Bluff—a long time. And she liked it. Moving her shoulders and smiling, she decided that she liked the feel of it. Unlike some of the other men whom she had fallen for or almost fallen for, she didn't have to make excuses for Nick, or rationalize why he did bad things to her. Nick needed no excuses and needed no rationalizations because he had never done anything bad to her. And thinking about it, she didn't see how he ever could. Not Nick. She couldn't see him ever doing anything to hurt her.

Now she wondered why she had never noticed him before. It was obvious that he hadn't noticed her. When she had first said hello to him shortly after he moved to the old Red Bluff, he didn't seem to recognize her. But they were both so different back then when she'd hang around the ranch house with Jenna, and Nick would be hanging around with Ryan. Plus she had grown her hair long. Back in those days, she had it really short. Being on the swim team, short hair made sense. After graduating college, growing it out seemed the natural thing to do. Shrugging, she finished combing her hair and began collecting the items that she'd need for school that day.

Her thoughts drifted back to Nick, which made her smile. She realized that she enjoyed thinking about him.

Then she thought that she should do something special for him for taking care of Jamie today. Cook him dinner? Well, she wasn't the greatest cook, but she could probably come up with something. Maybe a casserole, but she had never tried that in the wood cooking stove. Let's see, what ingredients would she need? Could she get them at Ralston General Store? Quickly checking the time, she was about to rush out the door when thoughts of Nick came rushing back to her.

What a great guy! Why did it take her so long to see it? Sighing deeply, she tilted her head unconsciously as images of him danced in her mind. Nick on the floor with Jamie, the three of them walking down the street holding hands, Nick there beside her when she told Jamie that his grandparents weren't going to return, Nick giving Jamie a balloon, and finally, Nick kissing her. At that moment, she knew that she would never want any other man in her life. He was the one for her—she was certain of that. And he was the perfect father for Jamie, too.

CHAPTER TWENTY-SEVEN

"THIS IS CALLED a truck, Jamie, and you'll have fun riding in it." Nick helped Jamie into the seat and secured the seat belt around him. Then he climbed into the driver's seat. "Are you ready?" When Jamie nodded, Nick started the engine. "You okay, buddy?"

Jamie held the handle on the door with one white fisted hand and nodded. "Yeah, I guess so."

Nick pulled out slowly. "I'm going to go faster now, but you're perfectly safe with me, okay?"

"Okay."

Nick drove to the thrift store, got out of the truck, opened the door for Jamie and helped him down, and handed him a quarter for the parking meter. "Here, Jamie. Put that in there. Yeah, like that."

Jamie jumped up and down. "More! I want to do it again!"

"We only need one, Jamie. We're not staying that long."

Nick held out his hand for Jamie, and they walked into the store together. While Nick was picking out clothes for Jamie, he didn't notice that Jamie wandered away from him. A minute later, Jamie was tugging at his sleeve.

"Come on over here and look at this, Nick. It looks cool." Jamie pulled on Nick's sleeve for him to follow.

"Cool, huh? Where'd you learn to say that?" asked Nick, holding onto the clothes that he had already picked out.

"From you!" Jamie walked him into a nearby corner that had shelves full of games. "Look! This one! Unc-le Wig-gy."

"Close. Uncle Wiggly. That's a fun game. I played it when I was your age."

"Can we get it, Nick? Please? Please?"

"Yes, but you have to do something for me first, okay?"

"What?"

"I want you to try these clothes on. Here is a fitting room. Go in, close the curtain, take your clothes off, put these on, and then let me see how they fit you. Okay?"

"Sure, Nick!" Jamie took the clothes from Nick's hands and disappeared into the dressing room. A minute later, he poked his head out from behind the curtain. "This shirt is too tight, Nick. I can't get it on."

"All right. Put the other shirt on, then, it's a little bigger. And put the jeans on."

Nick took Uncle Wiggly off the shelf and saw Chutes and Ladders above it, so he grabbed that game, too, and put them on the counter. He thought it would be fun for the three of them to play games. When Rachel came into his mind, he smiled.

The curtain opened, and Jamie walked out wearing jeans and a T-shirt that had a blue peace symbol on it. "They fit. Is this what children wear in this place?"

Nick laughed. "Yes, Jamie. That's what children wear."

He turned to the clerk. "Is it all right if he wears those out of here?"

"Sure. We can put his other clothes in the bag. Where are you from?"

Before he said "Red Bluff," he caught himself. "Oh, he's visiting from back East." Then, uncomfortable, he turned to Jamie. "Bring your other clothes out from the dressing room, Jamie."

Nick paid for everything, and he and Jamie walked back out to the truck. He looked at the dashboard clock and said, "We still have time before the dentist to bring Madison some orange juice. Let's go get some."

They stopped at a convenience store, and Nick picked up two half-gallon cartons of one hundred percent pure orange juice, one with pulp and one without. After paying for them, he drove back to the ranch house, walked in without knocking, and put the orange juice into the refrigerator. "Oh, Jamie. I should tell you about all this cool stuff in here, but there's no time now. Maybe later." Then he walked to the hallway and softly said, "Hey, Madison. You awake?"

"I heard the door and was hoping it was someone I knew. Yeah, Nick, what's up?"

"I brought you some orange juice and put it in the fridge. Hope you feel better! See you later!"

"Nick, I guess you're not the jerk that I thought you were! Thanks!"

Nick chuckled. "Thanks for the compliment, Madison. Bye."

As they walked out of the house and into the sunshine, Nick looked at Jamie. "It's almost time for the dentist, Jamie. Let's get you into the truck, and I'll tell you what's going to happen there."

When they arrived at the dentist, fifteen minutes early, Jamie understood that it might hurt for a minute, but then he wouldn't feel anything else. He wasn't happy about it, and he was scared, but Nick had told him what the carnival would be like, so he was excited about that. Nick thought that he might be more nervous than Jamie. The thought of Jamie hurting bothered him. It was almost like Jamie was his own son, and in a way, Nick felt like he was.

They called Jamie's name, and Nick walked up to explain that Jamie had never been to a dentist before. The nurse said, "It's okay, Mr. Gallanti, we'll take good care of him. Don't worry." And she put up her hand to keep him from following Jamie into the back. Nick had explained to Jamie earlier that he was going to have to be Jamie Gallanti and pretend to be his son so everything would work. Jamie had nodded solemnly and then brightened. "Can I call you Papa, then?" Nick had smiled at the boy and nodded. "Almost. You can call me Dad." Jamie liked that.

A half hour later, with Nick still pacing the floor worrying, the nurse escorted Jamie out. Jamie wasn't smiling, but he wasn't crying, either. "He'll be fine. Do you have any teething gel?" asked the nurse.

"Teething powder." Nick put his arm around Jamie, and Jamie pressed into him.

"I'll give you some sample gel. I'm sure that's all he'll need. It shouldn't hurt longer than one more day, I wouldn't think." The nurse handed him the gel along with the bill.

"Thank you." He handed her his credit card and turned to look at Jamie. "You okay, buddy?"

"I didn't like it."

Nick kneeled down and hugged him. "I'm sorry. But it should feel a lot better real soon, Jamie. Now we can go to the carnival! You ready?"

"I'm tired."

"Oh." Nick took his credit card and put it into his wallet. "Okay, come on. Let's go to the car."

"Will you carry me?"

Jamie looked up at him with such sad eyes that Nick couldn't help it. He scooped him up in his arms and kissed him on the cheek. "Come on, buddy. You'll feel better soon."

Nick wasn't sure what to do. Should they go to the carnival now, or should they go home and maybe he and Rachel could bring him back together? It was too early, anyway, so he drove to a shoe store that was close by and carried Jamie inside. He picked out a pair of rugged boy's tennis shoes with velcro fasteners and tried them on Jamie. "Can you stand up and walk around for me, Jamie? See how they feel on your feet?"

Jamie reluctantly stood up and walked around. "They feel comfortable." Then he sat down and tried to take the velcro off. "Show me how to do this." After Nick showed him, he pressed and pulled at the velcro until Nick finally made him stop. "Can I wear them?"

"Sure, Jamie. You want me to carry you again?"

"No, I'll walk."

Nick paid for the shoes and walked with Jamie back out to the truck. "What about now, Jamie? Do you want to go to the carnival?"

"I'm still kind of tired. Can we go home now?"

As excited as Jamie had been before about the carnival, Nick knew that he must not be feeling well to ask to go home. So he drove back to the ranch house, decided not to bother Madison again, and they rode Shiloh home to the old Red Bluff.

CHAPTER TWENTY-EIGHT

RACHEL RUSHED HOME from the store, putting the ingredients that she had bought on the counter, before rushing back out the door and across the street to the school. She still needed a pound of hamburger, but Ryan said he'd keep it and send someone over with it later, since she didn't have any way to keep it cold.

Walking into the schoolhouse, she wondered if teaching would feel any different now that she was in love. As she approached her desk, she didn't feel different. Maybe it was like when she turned twenty-one. She thought it would be this huge change, but the day afterward, it felt the same as being twenty. No big deal. The big deal, she thought, was in her head. And she liked the big deal about being in love. It was a wonderful feeling! Rachel was so happy about it, that it almost felt like her feet didn't touch the ground.

Everything for the day's class was prepared by the time the first kids started straggling in. Thinking about being in love with Nick and worrying about Jamie would both have to be set aside while she was at school. Focus! Focus! While she was struggling with focus, she noticed that Oscar slithered in the door. That alone was unusual. Normally, he walked in announcing his presence in a loud voice. Or sometimes he'd just walk in and shove a bigger kid to show his superiority. But he walked quietly in and stood beside his chair. When she took a closer look at him, he had an ugly red mark across his face. Oh, dear.

Not thinking, she said, "Oscar, why don't you go ahead and sit down."

His face didn't change at all. "I'd rather stand."

At first, she didn't understand, and she was going to ask him to sit again. But before the words came out, she realized why he didn't want to sit. If his face looked like that, no telling how bad his butt looked. And the mark on his face wasn't from a hand. His father hadn't slapped him—he had struck him in the face with the belt. Although she was still angry at what he had done to Jamie, she did feel sorry for the poor kid. As she watched him, he looked around and got a panicked look on his face. Then he walked up to her desk and whispered to her.

"Where's Jamie? Is he all right?"

Rachel nodded, but she had to collect her thoughts before answering. "Er, he's out of town today and will probably be back tomorrow or the next day."

"But he's all right?" asked Oscar again.

"Yes, he's okay." Rachel watched as Oscar nodded and walked away. She had never known him to show remorse before, so more than likely, his father had threatened him with more of a beating if Jamie was hurt. Regardless, she felt bad for the kid. Nobody deserves that kind of treatment.

Shortly before lunch, the classroom was disturbed by some commotion outside. Rachel sent an older boy outside to check it out. He ran back in, breathless, and shouted, "The stagecoach is leaving!"

When everyone stood up, ready to run outside, Rachel quickly said, "Everyone sit down. If you want to see the stagecoach leave—from here, we are not going to leave the school grounds—then you can stand up and walk out of here like the ladies and gentlemen that I know you can be." When everyone stood up and started walking out in an almost orderly fashion, Rachel said louder, "Stay up here on the school grounds!"

Rachel followed the children out and found all of them staying within ten feet of the school building—even Oscar. Usually, he would have ignored her and been the first one running down the street and shouting, with some of the others following. The beating must have impressed him. Still, she thought it was inappropriate. When the stagecoach was out of sight, Rachel said, "Kids, it's almost dinner time. So you might as well go in and get your dinner." Although she still thought of it as lunch, she tried to remember to call it dinner when she was at school.

Until the interruption from the stagecoach, Rachel had remained focused on school work. But with the kids outside eating their lunch, Rachel had more time to worry about Jamie and to think about Nick and her feelings about him. She wondered when they'd get back. Was Nick able to get an appointment for Jamie the same day, or would they have to stay there overnight? And now that she realized that she was in love with Nick, would it change anything between them? Would she act differently around him? Probably.

Remembering back to her boyfriend Michael, she shook her head. When she started acting differently around Michael, it was the beginning of the end. The image of that moment clarified in her mind. After she asked him to go to the party with her—a party he didn't want to attend—she had pleaded with him to go. And out of nowhere, his eyes clouded over and his hand raised and slapped her across the face. It was unexpected, and she was so stunned that she didn't know what to do. All she could do was stare at him while her face still stung from the slap.

After they had broken up, she always blamed herself for pushing him to that point. People had told her that it wasn't her fault—nice men didn't hit women. And yet she thought if she hadn't pushed him, then maybe he wouldn't have done that, and they'd still be together. Before that happened, she had the feeling he was going to ask her to marry him. Then it was over.

That was then. Michael was in her past. Nick was her future. Both her future *and* Jamie's future.

CHAPTER TWENTY-NINE

ON THE WAY home, Nick was so afraid that Jamie would fall asleep and fall off Shiloh, that Nick rode with one hand over Jamie's two hands that held onto him. They arrived back at the livery, and Jamie fell asleep leaning on the gate while Nick unsaddled the horse. When Ezra walked over and offered to brush Shiloh down, Nick accepted, picked Jamie up, and carried him back to Rachel's house.

After taking off Jamie's shoes, Nick put him on his bed, so he could finish his nap. Nick tilted his head and looked at the sleeping boy. His boy. He felt more and more like he was Jamie's father. And his next thought, naturally, was about Rachel. Thinking about Rachel always made Nick smile. His feelings for her were growing stronger, and now that he had gotten used to it, he decided that he liked it. Rachel. Rachel and Jamie. He wanted them both; he knew that now. He wanted to be Rachel's husband and Jamie's father.

The boy stirred in his sleep bringing Nick out of his reverie. There was no way to know how long he'd stay asleep, so Nick resigned himself to staying at Rachel's until he woke up. It had been a difficult trip for Jamie, what with the dentist, and all the new things about the future. So there was no telling when he might wake up.

Walking into the kitchen, Nick looked around. There were some items on the counter that looked like Rachel may have just bought them. Then he found the recipe for a casserole. All the ingredients for it were on the counter except the hamburger. Surely Ryan would have some hamburger tucked into his solar-operated cooler. When Jamie woke up, Nick would walk up there to see. If not there, maybe the hotel had some they could spare. If he could find the hamburger soon enough, maybe he could cook the casserole before Rachel got home and surprise her! Rachel usually skipped lunch, Jamie had been too tired to eat, and Nick was hungry, too. An early dinner—supper—would be perfect for all of them.

Nick paced back and forth in the house, checking Jamie's room every minute. Frustrated, he returned to the kitchen to check the recipe again. Yes, everything was there except the hamburger. When he heard something behind him, he turned around to see Jamie standing in the doorway rubbing his eyes.

"Nick? Can I go see my mama now? I want to show her my toof."

Nick kneeled down so they were face to face. "Does it still hurt, buddy?"

"It feels sore, but it doesn't really hurt. I just want to see my mama."

Jamie stood there and put his thumb in his mouth. Nick had never seen him do that and figured that he was still upset over his experience at the dentist. Still looking right at Jamie, he said, "Your mama's still at school, and I'd rather not disturb her. How about you go with me to the store so I can get something for dinner?"

"I'm ready for dinner now."

"Sorry, Jamie, I mean supper. But we'll get you a little snack at the store to tide you over, okay?"

"Okay." Jamie stuck out his hand to Nick.

"Let's put your shoes on first, shall we?" Nick pointed to Jamie's feet, and they both laughed.

After putting on Jamie's old shoes, Nick checked the recipe one last time to make sure the rest of the ingredients were there. Then the two of them walked up the street hand in hand, Jamie wanting to ask questions about the new Red Bluff, and Nick trying to explain how it had to be a secret.

Before they walked into the store, Nick put his finger to his lips to quiet Jamie. When they walked into the store, Bear greeted them, knocking Jamie over and licking his face. Jamie giggled and pushed the dog away.

"Hey, Ryan. I was wondering if you have any hamburger." Nick walked toward the counter where Ryan stood.

Ryan nodded. "Sure do. Is this for Rachel? She came by this morning asking about it, and I was holding it for her in the cooler."

"Yup. Jamie and I had to go to *town* today to see a dentist, and I thought I'd cook dinner before Rachel gets home."

"Yeah, Kat came by and mentioned that you had to take him. How'd he like it?" Ryan watched as Bear bowled Jamie over again, much to the boy's delight.

"He wanted to move there!"

"Oh, no! Not another one!" Ryan laughed.

Nick nodded. "I wanted to take him to the carnival that was there now, but he didn't feel good enough after seeing the dentist. Maybe another time. Anyway, can I buy the hamburger from you? I want to get dinner started."

"Supper." Ryan fished the hamburger out of the cooler and handed it to Nick. "Rachel already paid for it this morning."

"Thanks, Ryan. How about salad or vegetables? You have anything like that?"

"Yeah. Come look in the cooler." Ryan opened it up so Nick could peer in.

"Oh, this is perfect." Nick picked out two small heads of leaf lettuce. Then he picked up a cucumber, celery, some beets, an apple, and a few carrots. Reaching into his pocket, he pulled out only twenty-first-century money. "Oh, tarnation. All I have is the *other* money. Would you take that?"

"Sure, but you have to pay the other prices then." In a voice only loud enough for Nick to hear, he said, "Nineteenth-century money, nineteenth-century prices. Mostly because I need more nineteenth-century money and don't need twenty-first-century money. So, the answer is yes, but it'll cost you."

Nick frowned. "Well, it's all I have then, so here you go." He handed Ryan several bills. "Will this cover it?"

"Sure." Ryan nodded.

"Hey, I was wondering if I could borrow your wagon or go with you sometime when you go back there. I have something that I bought for Rachel, and I want to get materials to make her a composting toilet, too."

"Sure. How about Sunday? Mary Elizabeth usually goes with me, but this week she's going to her parents' for the day. I leave early in the morning. Would that work for you?"

"Perfect. I'll see ya then."

"So, Nick," Ryan leaned forward on the counter and said quietly, "is everything progressing with Rachel?" He raised his eyebrows.

"Thank you, Ryan! Good-bye! Come on, Jamie." Without answering, he walked swiftly to the door, pushed Jamie out the door in front of him, and left the store. Nick gave him the apple to eat on the way home.

When they arrived back at Rachel's house, Jamie played with his train in the bedroom while Nick got the fire going in the wood stove. Then Nick put a pan of water on the stove and waited for it to boil, so he could add the noodles. After they were cooked, he drained the water, put the rest of the ingredients into the pan, and placed it into the oven. There was nothing to do now except wait for Rachel to arrive. He walked into the bedroom, sat down on the floor with Jamie, and pushed the engine around the track.

CHAPTER THIRTY

THE AFTERNOON AT school dragged by for Rachel. She couldn't wait to get home to see if they were back. They had to be. And yet, what if they weren't? What would she do then? The concern about Jamie and Nick clouded her focus so she couldn't remember from one minute to the next what the kids were supposed to be doing. When the end of the day came, she wasn't sure who was happier—the kids or her. She strolled quickly across the street, pulled the door open with abandon, and was completely overwhelmed with the delicious smells that wafted to her from the kitchen.

There was Nick, standing in her kitchen wearing one of her old aprons, and preparing a salad. All the ingredients that she had left upon the counter were gone—no doubt in the wood cooking stove—because that's what it smelled like. Nick turned his head at her entrance and had a boyish grin on his face, as if he had been caught at something.

He shrugged. "I wanted to surprise you with supper. Hope it's okay."

"Oh, Nick. I was so worried about you and Jamie all

day." She fell into Nick's open arms, and Nick kissed her on the lips. A warm, welcoming kiss. "Where is Jamie? Is he all right?"

Jamie, standing in the doorway of his room, said, "I'm fine, Mama. Did you guys just kiss? Are you getting married?"

Without answering, Rachel broke from Nick's embrace, ran over, picked Jamie up, and swung him around. "Are you okay, big guy? How's your tooth?"

Jamie pulled down his lip with one finger showing Rachel the empty spot. "It's gone. It's still a little sore, though."

She hugged him. "Yeah, it might be for another day or so. I'm so glad you're all right, Jamie."

"I missed you, Mama."

"I missed you, too, sweetheart. I missed you a lot!" She stood up and kissed him on the top of his head.

Jamie ran back into his bedroom to play with his trains. Rachel turned back to Nick who was tossing the salad. "Thank you so much, Nick, for taking Jamie—and for this." She motioned to the salad, the beets cooking on top of the stove, and the delicious smells coming from inside the oven. "I wanted to cook dinner for you because of all you've done for me and Jamie."

"Too late! I wanted to cook *supper* for you. Since I figured that you'd worry all day, I thought it would be neat to surprise you with supper." He walked over and stuck a fork in the beets. "And I think everything is about finished."

Rachel turned and said, "I'll set the table." But when she looked, Nick had already done that, too. "You've thought of everything!"

"Go on, sit down. I'll go get Jamie and then bring

everything to the table."

Rachel, too stunned to argue, sat down with a smile on her lips. "Thank you, Nick."

"Sit down, Jamie. It's time for supper."

Nick put everything on the table and served everyone their food. "I hope you like it, Rachel."

"Nick, it's delicious! It's much better than when I make it. What did you do differently?"

"I found some spices in your cabinet over there." Nick motioned with his head. "Glad you like it!" He reached over and patted her hand.

"So how was your day today, Jamie?" Rachel looked at the boy and smiled.

"We went to this strange place, and they had—" Jamie put his hand over his mouth and looked at Nick. "I'm sorry."

Nick reached out and patted Jamie's hand. "It's okay, dude. Rachel is from *there*. She knows all about it. You can tell her everything."

Jamie's eyes got big. "You're from *there*?"

Rachel nodded. "Yes, Jamie. And so is Nick."

Jamie looked from one to the other astounded. "Really?"

"Go on with your story, sweetie. Tell me what happened."

Jamie went through all the details of his day, starting with going through the cave, using the toilet, the dentist, and getting new shoes. "See my new shoes? Aren't they cool?"

Rachel looked at Nick. "Cool, huh?"

"And we almost went to the carnival, but I was too tired! Can we still go? It sounds like a lot of fun! Please? I'm feeling better now! Please?"

"What carnival?" asked Rachel.

"Madison told us about it. It's in town this weekend. You want to go? The three of us?" Nick looked at Rachel.

"Yeah! That sounds like fun! But, Jamie, you have to keep it a secret, okay? Everything that we do *there* has to be a secret. Okay?"

"Yeah, I can keep it a secret. I promise." He looked from Rachel to Nick. "So, are we really going to go, then?"

"Yes, we are. Tomorrow!"

Jamie jumped up and ran around the house yelling, "We're going to a carnival! We're going to a carnival! Yippee!"

CHAPTER THIRTY-ONE

NICK HAD FINALLY convinced himself that he would do it. And it wasn't that he had to convince himself, it was that he had to override his fear of doing it. Of course it didn't help that he had never intended to do it, and the whole thought of it was new to him. But he had finally decided. He would ask Rachel to marry him—maybe at the top of the Ferris wheel. That would be memorable.

Climbing out of bed, he pulled on his jeans, cowboy shirt, and boots. After washing his face in the bowl of clean water, he dried it and raised one fist into the air. "Yes! I'm going to do it! Today's the day!" Then he sat at the desk waiting for Josiah to arrive, so he could leave.

After fifteen minutes of alternately pacing the floor, sitting at the desk, and gazing out the window, Nick finally saw Josiah ride by on his way to the livery. Nick ran out the back door to intercept him.

"Hey, Josiah, I'm taking off now, okay?" When Josiah nodded, Nick continued, "Everything is fine. Nothing came up. No news to report." The old Red Bluff was a quiet town in which not much happened. But he always felt the need to give a full report to Josiah. That was from his training with the new Red Bluff police force. A complete report—even a report on nothing—was required at the end of each shift. It was a hard habit to break.

"Okay, thanks, Nick. What's up? Where are you going in such a hurry?" Josiah asked.

"I'm taking Rachel and Jamie to the carnival in"—Nick hesitated—"you know."

"That boy will love it! Have a good time!" Josiah urged his horse forward toward the livery.

Nick walked back through the building and out the front door. Then he hurried down the street toward Rachel's house. When he knocked on the door, Rachel opened the door with a big grin.

"Hi, Nick! Jamie is so excited, I can barely contain him."

"You guys ready?"

"I'm ready. And Jamie's in the necessary. He should be finished in a minute."

Just then, the back door slammed open, and Jamie ran inside the house and, with his arms wide open, jumped onto Nick. Luckily Nick was ready for him and swung him around before putting him down. "I think you need to go close the back door, kiddo."

"Okay, Nick." Jamie ran toward the back of the house.

"Quietly!" said Nick.

"Okay." Jamie closed the door gently and walked back to where Nick was. "Are we going now? Are we? Are we?" He jumped up and down as he asked.

"Settle down, Jamie. Yup, we're going."

Nick took Jamie's hand and put his arm out for Rachel to put her arm through. They walked out the door, turned the corner, and strode toward the livery.

When they got there, the three of them stood looking at Nick's two horses. Rachel held out her hand and petted each of them on their noses.

Suddenly, Nick said, "Oh, no! I just thought of something. Rachel, do you have a horse?"

"No. Whenever I go—you know—I ride Dolly. But I know that Dolly has been at Jenna's ranch for a couple of days."

Nick winced. "Oh. How well do you ride?"

"Ah, mediocre at best."

"Oh no. Shiloh is my 'riding double' horse, but he's also my most gentle horse. And Cisco can't ride double, but he is also more for experienced riders."

Jamie had been standing in front of the horses, reaching up to pet them. He tugged on Nick's pants. "Nick! Nick!"

"Jamie, wait. This is a dilemma. I don't know what we're going to do."

Jamie tugged some more. "Nick! I have to tell you something. Cisco said he'd promise to be good."

"What?" asked Nick.

"Cisco said he'd promise to be good. He likes Mama, and he wants her to ride him."

Nick didn't say anything, but he closed his eyes, listening, then nodding. "Okay. Rachel." He put his hand on her shoulder and looked into her eyes. "Do you trust me?"

"Of course."

"Cisco can be a tough horse, but he promises to be gentle today. Are you willing to take the chance?"

With a big smile on her face, Rachel said, "Um, he told you that?"

"Yes, Mama! He told me that, too. I heard him. Can't

you hear him?"

Rachel looked at Jamie. "No, Jamie, I can't."

"Well, he said it. You have to trust Nick. Come on! I want to go to the carnival!" Jamie started jumping up and down again.

Nick shrugged. "Are you willing to try?"

Rachel nodded. "I guess so."

Just then, Ezra walked up to them. "You want a saddle, Nick?"

"I need both of them, Ezra. I'll come with you."

CHAPTER THIRTY-TWO

WHEN NICK GAVE her a leg up onto Cisco's back, Rachel was scared. She didn't know exactly what she expected the horse to do—maybe buck or something—but he stood still and didn't move at all until she urged him forward. At first as they walked along the road, she was tentative, but by the time they arrived at the cave, she felt more confident. The horse hadn't done anything wrong. Even when a deer ran out in front of them, he stopped, but didn't spook at all. He was as gentle as "he" promised.

When they arrived at the ranch house, Nick and Jamie took care of the horses, and Rachel knocked on the door. Zack answered and invited her in.

"Is Madison okay? Nick told me she was sick." Rachel followed Zack into the house.

"She's a little better today. Come see her. She's in the kitchen."

Rachel walked into the kitchen behind Zack. Madison sat at the table drinking a glass of orange juice and looking like she had been hit by a Mack truck.

Madison held up the glass of orange juice. "You can

thank Nick for me for this. I didn't realize he was so nice."

Rachel nodded and raised her eyebrows. "He is."

Madison said, "Oh! I didn't realize—"

"Well, it's still new. Kind of."

"I met your boy. He's darling. You'll have to tell me sometime how that happened. Oh! That reminds me. Zack, would you get Rachel that note that I left by the phone?"

Zack disappeared from the room and was immediately back, handing Rachel a note. She looked at it and squinted.

"Can you make it out? My handwriting is horrible," said Madison.

"It's from Lindy?"

"Yeah. She's a friend of yours, right? She said she had something important to tell you, and that she *needed* to talk to you."

Rachel turned toward the living room. "Can I use your phone?"

"Knock, knock!" Nick called from the other room.

"Knock, knock!" Jamie echoed.

"You ready to go, Rachel?"

Rachel turned back into the kitchen. "We need to leave now. We're going to the carnival." She stuck the note in her jeans.

"You're welcome to use the phone when you return— even if we're not home. Just come on in. 'Course, I still feel too rotten to go anywhere, but who knows. Oh, and don't knock. Just come in—in case I'm sleeping—you know. Bye."

"Thanks so much, Madison. Bye. Bye, Zack."

After all the good-byes, Nick, Rachel, and Jamie piled

into Nick's truck. After Nick buckled Jamie into the backseat and got in the truck, Jamie leaned forward and tapped Rachel on the shoulder.

"Be sure to put your seat belt on, Mama. Nick is a good driver, but you have to wear the seat belt to be safe."

Rachel and Nick looked at each other and smiled. "I know honey. I've got it on."

Rachel noticed that Jamie leaned back in the seat and relaxed. He trusted Nick. And so did she. When she glanced at Nick, she must have caught his eye, because he turned and smiled at her. Then he reached out and patted her hand.

"We're going to have a great time today! Even if we did have to come to the new Red Bluff to do it!"

"There's no carnival in the old Red Bluff, so I think we're allowed," Rachel said.

Nick laughed. "Yes, we're allowed!"

They pulled into the crowded parking lot; Nick locked the car, and they walked to the admission booth. Nick bought all of them an all-ride pass.

"Are you sure?" asked Rachel. "That might be too much for him."

"I think he'll be fine. Won't ya, kiddo?"

"I'm fime! I'm fime!" Jamie jumped up and down as Nick attached the blue bracelet around his wrist.

"Let's start slow. Where's the merry-go-round?" Rachel and Nick looked around until Nick spotted it. "There it is. Let's go!"

Nick grabbed Jamie's hand, Rachel grabbed Jamie's other hand, and they marched off toward the merry-go-round. After standing in line, Jamie climbed onto the merry-go-round and chose his horse: a big blue one with a black mane and tail. Its neck was stretched out to the right with its mouth open, and all four legs were stretched out as if it were running.

"This one! This one! I like it!"

"Jamie, you should choose a horse in the outside two rows. That one doesn't move," said Nick.

"No, I want this one!" Jamie insisted.

"Jamie, you will have more fun on one that moves," said Rachel.

Jamie, having never seen a merry-go-round before, didn't understand. "I want this one!"

Nick lifted him up, and Rachel climbed on the horse next to him, and Nick sat on the outside horse. When the merry-go-round started, and Jamie saw that Rachel's and Nick's horses moved up and down and his didn't, he said sadly, "My horse isn't moving, and yours are."

"Sweetie, we tried to tell you that." Rachel looked at him with compassion.

Jamie moved in the saddle as if trying to urge the horse forward. "I want to go up and down, too."

"Sorry, big guy. Not this time," said Nick.

When the merry-go-round stopped, big tears rolled down Jamie's cheeks, and he didn't bother to wipe them away. So they stood in line again, put him on a horse that moved, and he was happy again. "Can we do it again?" he asked.

"Let's try a different ride." Nick took his hand and walked toward the Ferris wheel.

They stood in line for a long time. While they waited, Nick picked Jamie up and placed him on his shoulders so he could look around. "Do you see anything you want to go on?"

"Yeah! That!" Jamie pointed to the flying saucers.

"Rachel?" Nick looked at Rachel with raised eyebrows.

Rachel pretended to put her fingers in her mouth as if she was retching. "I don't think so."

"Sorry, kiddo. That's not the kind of ride that your mama and I want to try. Do you see anything else?"

"That!" Jamie pointed to a food booth where kids were walking away carrying cotton candy.

"Ah! I was wondering when you would find that! Maybe after this ride." Nick put Jamie down as the line moved forward.

The three of them climbed into the seat together, with Jamie in the middle. Nick looked at Rachel and smiled. He put his arm on the back of the seat and patted Rachel's shoulder. The Ferris wheel moved, and they went up. Jamie tried to lean forward to look down, but Nick held him back. "Easy there, fella. Look that way." Nick pointed out in front of them as the wheel turned around.

"Wow! I can see forever!" Jamie shouted.

Nick looked over at Rachel as the wheel approached the top. "Rachel, you know that I really love Jamie." Rachel nodded. "And I also—" The wheel stopped abruptly.

"What happened?" asked Jamie with a shaky voice. "Are we going to fall?"

"No, buddy, we're fine." Nick looked back at Rachel, but the moment had passed.

Rachel had put her arm around Jamie and was trying to comfort him. "It's okay, Jamie. We're fine. Don't worry."

"I'm scared, Mama."

Rachel kissed him on the top of the head, glancing at

Nick, who looked off into the distance. What had he been about to say? The words she hoped to hear? The Ferris wheel moved, then came to a stop at the bottom, and the attendant opened the passenger compartment so they could get out.

CHAPTER THIRTY-THREE

NICK STAYED SILENT in the truck after they left the carnival. Jamie had gone on a fish ride, where little cars looking like fishes went on a gentle up and down path round and round. Then he rode on the boat ride, that had small boats floating and going around in a circle. Jamie kept honking the horn—it was so cute. And Jamie had eaten two packages of cotton candy, one hot dog, an order of curly fries, and an ice cream cone. Now, as they drove home, Jamie sat in the backseat with his hand on his stomach and softly moaning. Poor kid.

He had fun, though. After going on all the rides, he wanted to go on all of them again. Nick thought he would have another chance with Rachel at the top of the Ferris wheel, but the one jolt at the end had scared Jamie, so he didn't want to go on it again. Nick had to come up with something else now. And that had seemed so perfect. Oh, well. It wasn't meant to be.

He stole a glance at Rachel. Her head was turned to the back looking at Jamie. She wanted to rub his stomach, but she could only barely reach his knee, so she rubbed that instead.

"You're a really good mom," said Nick.

She smiled at him briefly, but her attention immediately went back to Jamie who still held his hand on his stomach. "You'll be okay soon, Jamie. I feel bad that I let you eat all that and now you feel sick."

"It's okay, Mama. I would have wanted to eat it anyway. And if we went back tomorrow, I'd eat it all again."

Rachel laughed at that. Nick smiled, but couldn't keep his mind off what he didn't do. He wanted her to be his so badly. Her and the boy. He wanted to be a family. And he still couldn't believe that his wonderful plan had fallen through. It would have been so perfect, so memorable.

Even after the aborted Ferris wheel try, Nick had enjoyed the day. The three of them had walked around holding hands. And at times, when Jamie ran ahead, Rachel and Nick held hands. It was a great time for all of them, and he knew that if they were married—if they were a real family—it would be great all the time. And he wanted great. He really wanted great.

As they approached closer to the house, Nick thought about the chair-desks in his horse trailer. Did the tarp cover them well enough? Did Rachel see them? He hoped not, because he wanted them to be a surprise. That and the composting toilet—although he had already told her that he'd make that for her. Wait until she sees the desks, though! Nick could hardly wait to see her face! It will be radiant; he just knew it. Rachel was everything that he had always hoped for in a woman—bright, sensitive, funny, compassionate. And she was such a great mother.

Since Nick had never wanted to get married, he had never considered what he would be like as a father. Now that he wanted to get married, he knew he would make a great father. A father to Jamie—and maybe one or two of their own. He already loved Jamie as much as if he were his blood. The kid was great, and Nick really cared about him.

When the truck turned into the driveway at the ranch house, Nick stole a quick peek at his horse trailer. It looked like the tarp covered everything very well. Rachel could not see anything except the blue tarp. Anything could be under it. She'd never guess that it covered something special for her classroom.

"Nick, would you mind taking Jamie with you while you get the horses ready? I need to make a phone call." She opened the back door of the truck, unhooked Jamie's seat belt, and rubbed his tummy. "Mama will see you in a few minutes, okay? Nick will take care of you."

When Jamie nodded, Rachel smoothed down his hair and walked toward the front of the house. Nick watched her go, reached inside the truck, and pulled Jamie out. "Come on, big guy. Let's go into the barn and get the horses. I'll carry you."

"I have a tummy ache, Nick." Jamie put his head on Nick's shoulder as they walked.

When they got into the barn, Nick found an empty stall with fresh straw on the ground, and gently lay Jamie down. "You wait there, okay, buddy? I'll be right here with Shiloh and Cisco."

As he tightened the two horses' cinches, he thought again about his abortive proposal attempt, and he frowned. It would have been so perfect! Now what would he do? He couldn't think of anything, and he hoped that he could come up with something original later. Although he felt bad, he would have felt a lot worse if he had known that he might not even get a second chance.

CHAPTER THIRTY-FOUR

RACHEL WALKED INTO the house without knocking as Madison had told her to. When she closed the door quietly behind her, she heard something in the other room. Madison called out, "Zack, is that you?"

"No, Madison, it's Rachel. I came in to make that call. Is that okay? Can I bring you anything?"

"Come here, Rachel."

When Rachel walked to the door of the back bedroom, Madison was sitting up in bed, propped up with a big pillow behind her, and reading a book. "You look a lot better than you did this morning."

Madison nodded. "Yeah, I feel better, too. Not great yet, but I'm mending. I should be able to go to school on Monday." She put a bookmark in the book and set it aside. "Listen, you are welcome to use the phone in Jenna's room—just to the left down there. You can close the door and have some privacy."

"Thanks, Madison. I'll do that. See ya later." Rachel walked down the hallway, into Jenna's room, and closed the door behind her. Then she pulled out the note from Lindy and tapped out the number. Rachel liked Jenna's phone—it was a speaker phone, and since the door was closed, Rachel decided to use it.

"Hello!"

"Hi, Lindy. I got your message. What's up?"

"Ray's out of prison."

"Oh, no. Has he contacted you yet?"

"No, but I expect him to any time now, and it's totally upsetting my life. Cody is finally out of therapy, and I know that if Ray comes back into our life, he'll have to go back in."

"Oh, wow."

"And Rachel, my life is so awesome right now. I got a promotion at work, I'm making good money, and everything is going great. I know that Ray is going to mess everything up for me again like he always does."

"Do you want him back?"

"No! A definite no! There's no way I'd take him back! I have no desire to return to the hospital! No more Ray —no more broken bones. I'm done with that jerk."

"I'm glad to hear that, Lindy. You took him back so often that I wasn't sure."

"Never again, Rachel. I can guarantee you that. But the reason that I called you is because—you know—you kind of disappeared. I was wondering if, maybe, if I need to, if you could help me disappear, too?"

"Lindy, yes, of course. If it comes to that, it won't be a problem. Just let me know. You can contact me here just like you did this time. And if it's an emergency, tell them that, and they'll let me know right away."

"Can't I have your new phone number so I can call you directly?"

"I don't have a new phone number, Lindy. I don't have any phone number. Sorry."

"Rachel, I don't know where you are, but if Ray starts pushing his weight around again, where you are sounds like the perfect place for me and Cody."

"Let me know, Lindy. You and Cody will be safe there."

"Okay, Rachel. Thank you. So what's going on in your life now? Oh, by the way, Michael told me to say hi."

"Oh, Michael! How is he? You know I sometimes wonder what would have happened if I hadn't pushed him that time. I've always blamed myself for him slapping me."

"Well, you can stop blaming yourself! Michael would have done it eventually, anyway. He just got out of jail for hitting his girlfriend. She's an idiot like I was—she bailed him out after she called 9-1-1 on him. Michael is like my dad—and Ray. It wasn't your fault at all."

"Oh, wow. Well, tell him hi, anyway. I'll never see him again."

"What else is going on with you, Rachel? You said you were teaching, right?"

"Yes, I'm teaching, and I love every minute of it. And I adopted a little boy—a six-year-old. Jamie. He's the light of my life."

"That sounds wonderful, Rachel!"

"And I've been seeing a man who is awesome. I think he's ready to pop the question, but you know men, so who knows? Anyway, I'm madly in love with him. He's waiting for me outside, so I better go. Don't hesitate to call if you need to, okay?"

"Thanks, Rachel. Congratulations on your little boy and your new man! Invite me to the wedding, okay?"

"Okay, bye!" Rachel hung up the phone and wondered how she could invite Lindy, because the wedding would certainly be in the old Red Bluff—if there *was* a wedding. Nick still had to ask her first.

She hung up the phone, opened the door, looked toward Madison's bedroom, and saw that Madison had fallen asleep, the book still in her lap. So Rachel walked silently down the hallway and out the door, closing it gently behind her.

On the way to the barn, Rachel wondered why Nick had been so quiet on the drive back. He had hardly said two words—even though he had been warm and wonderful at the carnival. The three of them had held hands, and sometimes just she and Nick held hands. She loved feeling like they were a family, and she wondered if he felt that way, too. And then she wondered if he really was going to propose to her, because he would be the perfect father for Jamie and the perfect husband for her.

CHAPTER THIRTY-FIVE

"Is HE OKAY?" Rachel pulled open the stall door and rushed to Jamie's side.

She had come up behind him, and Nick hadn't even known she was there until he heard her voice. "It's okay, Rachel. He's fine—except for his tummy ache. I wanted him to be comfortable while he waited."

"I'm okay, Mama. My tummy hurts, though."

"Are you okay to climb up on the fence, buddy? So you can get up behind me?" Nick asked.

Rachel helped Jamie to stand. "Do you think he's well enough to ride back? Maybe we should stay here."

"I can do it, Mama. I can ride. I want to go home."

Nick shrugged. "See, Rachel? He's fine. Come on, let me help you get on your horse, and then he can climb up with me." Nick helped her up and said, "You okay now?" When she nodded, he swung up onto Shiloh's back and reached for Jamie, who had climbed on the fence beside him. "Everybody ready? Let's go."

The ride home was quiet and peaceful. Nick still felt uncomfortable about not being able to propose to Rachel and still wondered about how he would do it. It distracted him enough that he didn't feel like talking. About halfway home, the movement of the horse seemed to put Jamie to sleep again, so he rode with one hand over Jamie's hands to keep him from falling off.

When they arrived at the livery, Ezra walked up from the back and offered to take care of the two horses. Nick picked Jamie up and carried him home, while Rachel walked beside him.

"Long day, huh, Rachel?" asked Nick.

"Yeah, I'm tired."

"Me, too."

Rachel opened the door to the house, and Nick carried Jamie into his bedroom, laid him on the bed, and took off his shoes. Then he leaned down and kissed him on the forehead. "Hope you feel better soon, buddy," he whispered.

He kissed Rachel gently on the lips at the door before walking outside. "Thanks for a great day, Rachel."

She smiled. "Thank you, Nick. You made it all happen, and it was great."

"Bye, now." Nick walked away and forced himself not to look back, although he felt like she was still watching him. He didn't even know why he did that. But he still felt off balance because of what happened—and what didn't happen—on the Ferris wheel. He had such high hopes that it was the correct moment, and then everything fell apart. When he walked into the sheriff's office, he was still frowning.

"Hey, Nick. Did you have a good time at the carnival?"

"Yeah, it was great," Nick answered without enthusiasm.

"Hmmmm." Josiah straightened the wanted posters

on the desk and then stood up.

"Listen, Josiah. I've been spending some time with Rachel on some evenings, but I never asked you about it. Is that okay—I mean, if something happened in town, do you think they could find me?"

Josiah laughed. "Nick, the whole town knows exactly where you are. They know all about you and Rachel."

Nick felt himself blush. "Well"—he sat down at the seat that Josiah had vacated—"I guess it's time for me to make it official then."

Josiah, at the door, turned quickly to look at Nick. "What? Really? When are you getting married?"

Nick looked up at him, elbows on the desk and chin resting in both his hands. "I don't know." He sighed. "I was going to ask her today, but it got all messed up. Now I have to figure something else out. I want it to be memorable."

"Memorable? Nick! Dude! You're asking that woman to marry you! That's memorable enough!"

"I want something special for Rachel. And the idea I had for today didn't work out, so now I have to come up with something else."

"Oh, Nick. *You* are special! You're going about this all wrong, man. Just do it! She will be so excited, and that's enough. She does want to marry you, doesn't she?" Josiah raised his eyebrows.

"Well, yeah, I think so. We get along great. And sometimes she looks at me with that look—you know that look that women sometimes give you—*that* kind of look. I'm pretty sure she does. And I know that she likes the way that I am with Jamie."

Josiah stood in front of the desk. "Listen, man, I'm telling you. Just do it. Don't wait. Go on back over there right now! I can stay. Go ask her now. Honest, it's the right thing to do." He shook his head. "Sometimes it's bad to wait, Nick. Do it now."

"Thanks, Josiah, but I need to do it my own way. Bye."

Josiah walked out of the office and closed the door behind him. Nick, having nothing else to do, leafed through the wanted posters that he had been through a hundred times before. Maybe he should have listened to Josiah and just gone and asked her. No, that's not what he wanted to do. He wanted it to be special for her. Really special. Rachel was awesome, and he wanted something as special as she was. He'd wait. And the following day he'd go to town with Ryan and get the chair-desks and the materials to make her the composting toilet. She'd like that.

CHAPTER THIRTY-SIX

IT HAD BEEN a long day—a great day—but long. When Nick left, she watched him walk halfway up the street, and then she was too tired to watch him go any farther. After checking on Jamie, who was still sleeping soundly, she walked into her bedroom, fell onto the bed with her clothes still on, and fell asleep.

When she woke up, it was the middle of the night. She used her flickering flashlight—to simulate a candle in case anyone was looking in—to use the necessary and then take off her clothes and get into her nightgown. It occurred to her when she lay back down to sleep. Nick hadn't kissed her! Well, yes, he gave her a peck on the mouth, but not a *real* kiss like she was used to. And he had been quiet on the way home. And he never waved to her after he walked away. He *always* waved to her after he walked away! What had she done wrong?

Rachel had gotten enough sleep to ease her fatigue, but now, worrying about what she might have done wrong kept her awake. Going over every possible minute of the day, wondering if it had been this word or that sentence or was it even something that she had said?

Maybe it was something that she did or didn't do. Should she not have used the phone at the end of the day and left Nick alone with an ailing Jamie? Maybe Nick thought that she was a bad mother because of that. Although he had just said that he thought she was a good mother. That was before she had left him at the end of the day. What had she done to upset everything? Just when she thought that he was going to propose, and now she had spoiled it.

She finally fell asleep not long before Jamie came in and bounced on the bed. "Mama! Mama! I feel good today! And I'm hungry!" He knelt down and put his face right in front of hers. "I'm hungry, Mama!" Then he started jumping up and down again. "Come on! Time to get up! Let's go to the carnival again! I want cotton candy for breakfast!"

Rachel pulled him down beside her and cuddled with him. "Cotton candy, huh? Didn't you get sick enough yesterday?"

"I won't eat as much today," he said in a matter-of-fact manner.

"I don't think so, little one. What kind of mother would I be if I gave you candy for breakfast?"

"A good one!"

"I think we'll have oatmeal for breakfast. Sorry, kiddo." Rachel moved away from him and jumped out of bed.

"Oatmeal!" Jamie jumped up and down on the bed. "Oatmeal!"

After they finished breakfast and Rachel got them both dressed, she took Jamie's hand and walked out the door on her way to the hotel. She needed to arrange the next week's lunches, because she still wasn't up to making lunch every day on top of everything else that she had to do. There was a moment's hesitation when she considered whether or not that made her a bad mom, but then she realized that the lunches that Granny had been providing were nutritious and probably better than she would make herself.

It was early, so they walked in quietly, because Rachel didn't want to wake anyone who might still be sleeping. She heard voices and laughter coming through the door that led to the restaurant. Smiling, she was about to step through when she heard Josiah's voice say, "Nick said, '*I'm* not the marrying kind!'" The laughter coming from the people Josiah was talking to chilled her. As she rushed back out the door, she heard Josiah say, "And then —" She was out the door and running down the street, tears streaming down her face, still holding Jamie's hand with him running and trying to keep up with her.

Rachel opened the door of her house, dropped Jamie's hand, and threw herself onto her bed, still crying. "What's wrong, Mama? What's wrong?" Jamie rubbed her on the back. "Tell me, and I'll make it all better, Mama. Please tell me."

Rachel put her arms around him and said, "Thank you, Jamie." As she sat on the edge of the bed, holding Jamie, she felt so grateful that she hadn't heard the rest of what Josiah was going to say. "And then—" What would it have been? "And then Nick said that the last person that he would ever think of marrying—if he *was* the marrying kind—would be Rachel." She sighed, and the tears fell silently down her face again. She couldn't stay here; she knew that. Leaving was the only option after what happened yesterday and what she heard today. If she couldn't find a teaching job in the new Red

Bluff, then she'd get a job waitressing, like she did when she was in college. Not a big deal. She was out of here.

What about her teaching job in the old Red Bluff? Who would take it over for her? Maybe Mary Elizabeth could take over for her until she figured out what she was going to do. "Let's go, Jamie." After drying her tears and putting cold water on her face, she stepped out her door, holding Jamie's hand, and walked toward the livery—she wanted to go the back way to the store, so she wouldn't have to walk past the sheriff's office. Nick would certainly be in there sitting in that chair and maybe looking out the window.

As she turned the corner, at the other end of the street, she saw a wagon turning the corner by the store. Although she wasn't sure, it looked like it might have been Ryan and Nick. At least she didn't have to worry about running into him now. Opening the back door of the store, she called in, "Knock knock! Anybody home? Can I come in?"

"Come on in, Rachel! I'll be right down!"

When she heard Mary Elizabeth's voice, she felt relieved. "Come on, Jamie," and she pulled him inside. Bear ran down the stairs with a clatter and ran up to Jamie, who knelt down to avoid being jumped on again.

"Hi, Mary Elizabeth," Rachel said when she saw her. "I have a huge favor to ask."

Mary Elizabeth put out her hand and touched Rachel's face. "Have you been crying?"

Rachel shrugged it off. "It's nothing, really. I was wondering if you would mind taking over at school for the next few days. I need to get out of town."

"What is it, Rachel? Come on, we're friends."

Rachel shook her head, and tears started to fill her

eyes again. Not looking up, she said, "Please, Mary Elizabeth. Say you'll do it."

"I wish you'd tell me what's happened, but sure, I'll do
it. Granny doesn't need me this week, and Ryan will be
fine without me. No problem."

"Okay, thanks. Bye." Rachel headed for the door.

"Rachel, I really wish you'd tell me—"

Jamie stood up and pushed Bear away so he could
follow Rachel. "It was at the hotel—"

Rachel grabbed him by the arm and pulled him out
the door before he could finish. Then she rushed down
the street toward the livery. "Ezra! Ezra!" When Ezra
came out smiling, she said, "I don't know if you can help
me, Ezra, but I need a gentle horse that can ride double.
And I need him for at least a few days—I'm going, um,
out of town, if that's okay."

"I just got a new horse in, Rachel. He's a real sweetheart and pretty, too. A white speckled horse. His name
is Snowman. Would you like to see him?"

"No, if you think he'll be okay for us, then I'll take
him. I'll be right back."

And she rushed out the door to her house. With Jamie
riding behind her, she couldn't wear a backpack. So she
tried putting on some clothes—on top of each other—
that she didn't want to leave behind, and dressed Jamie
in the twenty-first-century clothes and shoes that Nick
had bought him. Nick! She didn't even want to think his
name. Then she pulled out a big purse, and she stuffed in
some underwear and everything else that she thought
might fit and put it over her shoulder, hanging in front of
her. That would work.

When she returned to the livery, Ezra had the horse
saddled and waiting for her. He helped her up on the

horse, then lifted Jamie up behind her. And she was off, up the road and toward the cave. She would miss the old Red Bluff—she did love it here—but sometimes a person just doesn't have a choice. And although she never considered how she was going to handle having Jamie in the new Red Bluff, she knew everything would work out. It had to. Her life in the old Red Bluff was finished. She couldn't return.

CHAPTER THIRTY-SEVEN

NICK HAD FINALLY recovered from his abysmal failure of the previous day's attempt at proposing to Rachel. Although he hadn't yet come up with a new way to ask her to marry him, he knew that he'd come up with something eventually. And the way that he felt about Rachel —he hoped that it would be soon. But he was grateful to be in the wagon with Ryan, heading toward the new Red Bluff, where he was going to buy the materials to build the composting toilet for her and to bring home the chair-desks. He thought both of those would please her. And he could hardly wait to see her face when she walked into the classroom and saw the chair-desks all in place.

When he thought again about the day before, and how much fun they all had, and how much they had felt like a *family*, Nick almost wept with how perfect it all was. Rachel and Jamie meant more to him than anyone that he could ever think of. Had he ever felt this way about anyone before? He didn't think so. And he liked the feeling—he liked being part of something that was bigger than himself. A family. What a wonderful feeling it was.

Nick could barely remember when he last felt like he had a family. When he was a troublemaking kid, they gave him no support. And when he straightened out and decided on becoming a cop, they still gave him no support. They had made fun of him and continually told him that he'd never make it, and that he would go back to causing trouble. Although he had proven them wrong, it hadn't given him any satisfaction. He didn't even invite them to his graduation from the university or from the Police Academy. They didn't even know for a long time that he was a cop, until he had stopped his father for speeding and given him a ticket.

It was a good thing that he never had any thoughts of reconciliation, because after that, there wasn't a chance in hell—those were the words that his father had said to him. And Nick didn't care. Getting away from that family was the best favor he could have done for himself. They had subtracted from his life rather than added to it. He wouldn't have put up with their behavior if they were friends, so why would he put up with it because they're family? His was a toxic family and better off left behind.

It made him wonder about Rachel. She never mentioned her family, and she would go weeks at a time, maybe even months, between her trips to the new Red Bluff. It didn't seem like she had anyone there who was important enough to her to keep in constant contact with. Perhaps Rachel longed to have a family again, too.

Nick thought that the whole line of reasoning was so ironic. For years, he had said that he didn't have a family, and that he didn't need one, either. Now, suddenly, he gets a taste of what a real family feels like, and he can't wait to have one. He never thought that he was either husband or father material, and now he felt strongly that he would be good at both. And he felt certain that Jamie would feel that way. He was pretty sure about Rachel, but not positive. Nick had found that one could never be certain where a woman was coming from. Of course, that was part of the mystery about them that he loved.

"Nick? *Nick*! Where are you, dude? You haven't heard anything I've said!" Ryan gave Nick's shoulder a shove.

"Oh, sorry, Ryan."

"Are you thinking about Rachel again? Man, you *do* have it bad, don't you?"

"I prefer to think of it like I have it good, Ryan."

"So what are you going to do about it?"

"Marry her, if she'll have me. We'll be a family—she and I and Jamie. I love that kid, and I love her."

Ryan slapped Nick on the back. "Congratulations, Nick! I've never been happier than since I married Mary Elizabeth."

"She hasn't said yes, yet." He smiled at Ryan. "But I'm pretty sure that she will. We get along great and always have a good time together."

"I'm so happy for you, Bro." Ryan shook the reins to speed up Dolly. "Oh! You're both from the new Red Bluff, so where will you get married?"

"We may both be *from* the new Red Bluff, but we both live in the old Red Bluff now, so I'm sure it will be there —unless Rachel wants it otherwise. It doesn't matter to me. I just want to please her. She means the world to me, Ryan. She means the world to me."

CHAPTER THIRTY-EIGHT

WHEN THEY ARRIVED at the barn, Rachel had Jamie climb onto the fence and then onto the ground. Then she got off the big, speckled horse. After putting him into a stall, she made sure that he had hay and water, and then she took Jamie's hand and walked tentatively toward the house. Rachel felt relieved when she saw that both Zack's and Madison's cars were gone. Good, she thought. She wouldn't have to talk to anyone about her decision. But she still had to leave a note about the horse. Although she didn't know exactly what was going to happen, she did know that she wouldn't return to the old Red Bluff to collect the rest of her belongings for at least a few more days.

Opening the door hesitantly, she called inside, "Anybody home?" There was always the chance that one of them were home and the car was elsewhere. But nobody answered, so she found a piece of paper by the phone, hurriedly wrote a note about taking care of the horse, and then put it in the middle of the kitchen table, under a salt shaker, so they would be sure to see it.

Pulling Jamie with her, Rachel rushed out of the

house and around the back to where she parked her car. Since she didn't return to Red Bluff often, her car was in an out-of-the-way spot. She had to drive it over a curb and out through the neighbor's driveway. But she was free—out from any encumbrances from her former nineteenth-century way of life. If she could talk Zack, Madison, Jenna, or someone into getting the rest of her belongings, she might never have to return there, which was fine with her. She was sure she could get Zack to return the pretty speckled horse for her.

The horse was everything that Ezra had said about him, gentle and responsive, too. He was the kind of horse that she might have considered buying for herself, had she stayed in the old Red Bluff. That was past history now; it wasn't going to happen.

When Nick came to mind, she fought the image of him away. How could she have been so stupid to fall for a man like Nick? He wasn't a family man; that much was obvious. Not the marrying kind, Josiah had said. What a jerk. She glanced over at Jamie. What she felt worse about was the relationship that Nick had formed with Jamie. Now how was Jamie going to feel? She thought that Nick was even more a jerk because of what he had done to Jamie. After Jamie's father dying, his grandfather abandoning him, and now Nick—Jamie might never be able to trust another man. Tears rolled down her face, and although she tried to control her crying, it soon developed into great heaving sobs.

"Mama? Mama, what's wrong?" asked Jamie, concerned.

Rachel sniffed, then reached over and patted him on the hand. "I'll be okay, Jamie. Don't worry. I'll be fine. We'll be fine." She took big gulping breaths, trying to get control of her breathing.

"Why are we here, Mama? Are we going to the carnival again?" Before Rachel could answer, Jamie added, "No, we can't be going to the carnival, or Nick would be going with us. Where are we going, Mama?"

"We're going to meet your grandmother."

"Grammy? And Grampie?" He moved up and down as much as the seat belt allowed him.

Rachel reached out to him. "Oh, Jamie, I'm sorry, no. This is my mother—who is now your grandmother, too. We might be staying with her for a while."

"You mean we're not going home?" Jamie turned to look at her, and Rachel could see a serious expression on his face. "I want to go home! I want to see Nick!"

She tightened her mouth and her voice grew hard. "I'm sorry, Jamie. We're done with Nick."

"I don't want to be done with Nick! I love Nick! I want to go see Nick!" Tears streamed down his face.

Her voice softened, and she patted his arm. "I'm sorry, Jamie. We can't see Nick anymore. I'm sorry."

"I want to go home! I want to go home and see Nick!" His tears turned into sobs.

"This is home now, Jamie. We're going to live here," she said soothingly.

"No! I'm going home! I'm going home to see Nick!"

He pushed the button on the seat belt, and it snapped open. Then he grabbed for the handle of the door, but before he could open it, Rachel had grabbed him. She pulled over to the curb, slammed the car in park, undid her seat belt, and pulled him to her.

"Oh, Jamie. I love you so much, and I don't want anything to happen to you. Please don't ever do anything like that again. Cars can be dangerous. You could have been hurt." Kissing him on the top of the head, she added, "I love you, Jamie."

"I want Nick, Mama. I want Nick."

"So do I, honey, but he doesn't want us. That's the sad truth of it. We want him, but he doesn't want us."

"Yes, he does, Mama. Nick loves us just like we love him. I know it, Mama. I know he does."

She rocked him as well as she could in the small car. "If only it were so, Jamie. If only it were so. Come on, now. Let's buckle you back up and get you to your new grandmother's house. She's going to love you, you little munchkin!" She kissed him on the tip of his nose and refastened his seat belt, then she put the car in drive and drove down the street.

CHAPTER THIRTY-NINE

NICK ENJOYED HIS time spent with Ryan talking about sports, old girlfriends, and bantering back and forth about what it will be like to be two old, married men. But anytime Ryan was busy—picking up items for the store—Nick's thoughts would race back to Rachel. It was like she—and Jamie—were his whole life now. He felt absolutely consumed by them—in a good way. He loved how it felt, and he could hardly wait to make it official. Although he still hadn't come up with an inventive and memorable way to ask her to marry him, it was beginning not to matter. There was a chance that he would ask her next time he saw her, no matter where it was. Because he now realized that however and wherever he proposed, it would be perfect.

"Come on, Nick. Stop dreaming and help me get this stuff into the cooler." Ryan came up behind him and opened the door to the truck.

Nick felt a little bad that Ryan couldn't buy as much as he wanted to because Nick's purchases would fill most of the wagon for the ride home. But somehow Ryan managed to stuff more food in the cooler than Nick had thought possible.

"It's like a jigsaw puzzle, that's all—or maybe Tetris. Anyway, I've been doing it for a while now, and I've gotten good at it. I'll get everything you want in the wagon, too, although at first it won't look like it will all fit. Let's go to the hardware store and get the materials for the composting toilet. I'm ready to get back home. I don't like being away from Mary Elizabeth this long. I'm used to her coming with me." Ryan put his hands on his hips and scowled at Nick. "Aren't you going to make fun of me for saying that?"

Nick chuckled. "No, I can hardly wait to get back to town so I can go see Rachel!"

As they were loading everything in the back of the pickup, a woman walked by, stopped, and said, "Ryan! Nick! Hello, you two!"

"Hi, Mary," said Ryan.

"Hello, Mary," said Nick.

"Haven't seen you boys in a while," she said, then looked up at a man gesturing from the front of the store. She rolled her eyes. "I'm being paged. See you later!" And she ran off toward the front of the store.

They finished loading their purchases and hopped into the truck. As they drove away, they glanced at each other and both said simultaneously, "She still looks really pretty, but not as pretty as—" and they ended the sentence with "Mary Elizabeth" and "Rachel" respectively. Then they high-fived each other and started laughing so hard that Nick had to pull over. When the laughter had subsided, Nick noticed that they were in front of a drug store. "Do you mind? I want to run in and get a stuffed animal for Jamie. It will only take a minute. Do you mind?"

"Go ahead." Ryan took a small notebook and a pen from his pocket and began marking off his list.

Five minutes later, Nick returned with the bear that he had picked out. Ryan took it out of the plastic bag and nodded. "Yup. This is cute. Jamie will like that."

"I think so, too."

Nick started the truck, and they drove off toward the ranch house. When they got there, Nick backed the truck up toward the gate where Ryan had parked the wagon.

"Let me put the cooler in first, then we'll work on everything else. Your chair-desks will be last." Ryan slid the cooler into his nineteenth-century box that hid its newness. "Okay, it's in. Start handing me the small stuff, first." When that was in the wagon securely, Ryan asked for the lumber. When he had it all situated, he said, "Okay, let's load the desks into the pickup, so we don't have to carry them all the way over here."

Twenty minutes later, everything was piled onto the wagon and held into place by rope. Nick's stomach was starting to turn circles thinking about seeing Rachel and asking her to marry him. Now that he had decided to just do it, he couldn't wait to get it done. He hadn't bought a ring first, because he thought that if Rachel was going to be the one wearing the ring, then she should pick it out herself. And he hoped that she would be pleased with that.

The ride home felt like it took longer than usual, but Nick thought it was because he was so eager to get there. They stopped in front of the store and managed to unload all the lumber from under the chairs. Ryan had arranged it so that it was easy. Then Ryan pulled into the livery, Nick asked about keeping the desks in a stall, and they unloaded them.

"Oh, shoot!" Ryan shook his head, grimacing. "I forgot to unload the cooler. I can usually do it myself, but I loaded it up extra heavy today. Would you mind helping me carry it back to the store? I know you're rarin' to go, but it will only take a few minutes."

"Sure, Ryan. No problem." As they walked out the front of the livery with the cooler, covered with an old saddle blanket, Nick glanced down the street toward Rachel's house. In a few minutes, he'd be at her front door. He sighed in anticipation.

They carried the cooler into the store, and Ryan said, "Thanks a lot, Nick."

"I'm the one who owes you thanks for taking me today and carting back all my stuff. Thank you! Now I'm going to run over to Rachel's! Jamie is going to love this little bear!" He pulled the bear out from beneath his shirt where he had stuffed it. Then he opened the back door.

Before he had a chance to step through it, though, he heard Mary Elizabeth call, "Nick! Nick, wait!" But Nick was too excited to wait a minute more, and he rushed out the door and ran down the street toward Rachel's house.

As he stood in front of her door holding the teddy bear, he had a huge grin on his face. When she didn't answer right away, he knocked again. After a few more minutes, he knocked again. That was strange. Should he just walk in to make sure everything was all right? He wasn't comfortable doing that, and then the thought of Mary Elizabeth calling to him came to mind. Maybe something had happened to Rachel—or Jamie—and that's what Mary Elizabeth was going to tell him.

Nick raced up the street to the store and entered through the back door without knocking. Ryan and

Mary Elizabeth were standing at the bottom of the stairs talking.

Mary Elizabeth walked over to him and put her hand on his arm. "I'm sorry. I tried to catch you before you left, Nick. Rachel's gone."

CHAPTER FORTY

WHEN THEY ARRIVED at her mother's house, Rachel turned off the engine and stayed in the car for a minute breathing. She hadn't seen her mother in months. How would her mother react? Certainly she would let them stay, wouldn't she? She and her mother had never gotten along. Rachel's earliest memories were of her mother picking on her for one thing or another. And it only got worse after her father died. She didn't often visit her mother because every time she saw her, her mother would say something to set Rachel off, and then Rachel would just leave. But she wouldn't do that around Jamie, would she? Her mother would treat him like the wonderful little boy that he was—at least Rachel hoped that she would do that. Her mother had always been unpredictable, although her moments of loving warmth had never been a common occurrence.

Jamie unhooked his seat belt himself and was reaching for the door handle when Rachel stopped him. "Listen, buddy." She put her hand on his arm, holding him in place. "Let's make a deal. This is a dangerous place for little boys. Remember when you almost got run over by the stagecoach horses?" Jamie nodded. "Well, you could get run over by cars, and it would be much worse. And there are a lot of cars here. So, let's make a deal, okay? From now on, I will unhook the seat belt and open the door when *I'm* ready for you to get out. I love you, and I don't want anything to happen to you. Okay? Is that a bargain?"

Jamie, tears staining his face, nodded. "Okay, Mama. I promise."

Rachel walked around to the other side of the car, opened the door, and helped him out. "And anytime we're around cars, you'll hold my hand."

He looked up at her and smiled. "I'll hold your hand anytime, Mama!" Then his smile faded. "But I'd like to hold Nick's hand, too." Tears streamed down his face again.

Rachel knelt down and wiped the tears away. "We can talk about that later, okay? Let's go meet your new grandmother now. It's not the time to cry."

Jamie sniffed and ran a hand across his nose. "Okay, Mama."

Rachel took a deep breath and plastered a smile across her face. She realized that her need to do that was telling. But where else would she go? They walked up to the front door, and she knocked, trying to maintain her smile.

The door opened, and her mother had a sneer on her face. "Well, look what the cat dragged in." A cigarette dangled from her mouth, and she stood there, blocking the way without moving.

Rachel shrugged. "Aren't you going to invite us in?"

"Yeah, sure, if I *have* to. But I'm not putting out my cigarette for the little rug rat. I just lit it, and I'm not

183

wasting it. Who is he, anyway?"

"He's my son. This is Jamie. Jamie, this is your grand-mother."

"Hallo, Grandmother." Jamie stuck out his hand, and she pushed it away.

"Your son? That was quick. How'd that happen?"

"He's adopted, Mother, obviously."

"Yeah, well, whatever." She pointed her hand with the cigarette at Jamie. "Don't call me grandmother. *I'm* not your grandmother."

"Okay, I won't." Jamie looked up at her and tears started streaming down his face again.

"Oh! Now the little brat is a crybaby. Why didn't you pick one that didn't cry?"

"Mother, I was wondering if we could stay here for a while—until I find a job." Rachel couldn't believe that she was begging her mother to stay in a place where she knew that she—and Jamie—would be verbally abused. Constantly.

"Stay here? You and the little crybaby brat? I thought you already had a job." She smashed her cigarette out in an ashtray and lit another one in the same motion.

"It didn't work out. Can we stay here or not?"

Jamie pulled on her hand until her face was even with his. "Mama, I don't want to stay here. She's mean. She's not nice to me or you."

"What did the little brat say?" She looked at Jamie. "Speak up, crybaby! Let the whole world hear!"

"He said that he doesn't want to stay here because you're mean. And I agree with him. Good-bye, Mother." Rachel walked to the door, opened it, and the two of them walked out the door.

Her mother opened it and called after them, "And

don't come back!" Then she slammed the door behind her.

Rachel buckled Jamie into the seat belt and stepped into the car before she broke down completely. Sobbing, she held her hands over her face, while Jamie stroked her arm.

"It's okay, Mama. It's okay. She was mean to us. We don't have to stay here with her. It's okay, Mama."

Rachel took a deep breath and looked at him. "You're absolutely right, Jamie. We don't have to. I don't know where we can go, but we don't have to put up with that kind of treatment from anybody. How'd you get so wise for six years old?"

He shrugged and leaned over to kiss her on the cheek. "Can we go home now? To Nick?"

"No, I'm sorry, Jamie, we can't." Although she could see that he quietly wept on his side of the car, she didn't want to explain any further. How could she? Nick wasn't what she wanted to think about right now. She had to find them someplace to stay. Where could that be? Lindy! She could call Lindy!

Rachel drove to a gas station to use the pay phone on the corner of the property. Since everybody had cell phones, pay phones were outmoded now—but she had given up her cell phone when she moved into the past. There were still a few pay phones around if you looked hard enough. She dug in her pocket for some coins and realized that they were all nineteenth-century coins. They would still work in the phone, but while she never expected to return to the old Red Bluff, she wasn't going to use them. They would be worth some money, and she might need that money until she found a job.

She pulled out her charge card that she had kept in

185

her desk at her house in the old Red Bluff, and asked the operator to connect her. While she waited, she looked in disgust at the phone booth. It was filthy—people had used it for a garbage can. There were soda cans all over the floor, and it smelled like somebody had urinated in it. A large spider hung in a web across the top corner, so Rachel tried to stand under the opposite corner. When she heard Lindy answer, Rachel said, "Lindy! It's Rachel. Any chance I can stay with you for a few days? And I have my son with me."

CHAPTER FORTY-ONE

THE TEDDY BEAR was still in Nick's hand. When Nick heard Mary Elizabeth's words and saw the sad expression on her face, he inadvertently clutched the teddy bear to his chest. "What do you mean 'she's gone'?"

Mary Elizabeth shook her head slowly and walked back to stand beside Ryan. "I don't know. She asked me to fill in for her at the school for a few days."

Nick felt hope rising. "You mean she'll be back in a few days, then?"

"I don't think so, Nick. She said a few days, but I had a feeling that she was done. She'd been crying."

"Why? Why was she crying? What happened? Was Jamie okay?" Nick sank into the chair that was in front of Ryan's latest painting.

"Jamie was fine. That's not what it was. I don't *know* what it was, but she looked utterly defeated, like she had lost her only friend in the world."

"Was it something I did or said?" Nick looked at her, hoping that wasn't it.

"I don't know, Nick. I honestly don't know anything more."

187

"But where would she go?"

"I'm sure she went *there*."

"How would she get there? We had Dolly." Nick had the teddy bear in his lap, and he kneaded it between his hands, while Bear stood by hoping that he'd drop it.

"I don't know, Nick. I just don't know."

Nick stood up. "I'll go check with Ezra. See if he knows anything." He slunk out the door with his head hanging down and his spirits even lower.

"Ezra! Ezra!" he called as he walked into the livery.

"Hey, Nick. You going riding this late? Whose saddle do you want me to bring you?"

"No, Ezra, no. Have you seen Rachel?"

"Yeah, this morning. She rented a gentle horse from me—a big, strong, gentle fellow named Snowman."

"Did she say where she was going?"

Ezra nodded. "Yeah, she said she needed him to go out of town for a few days."

"Okay," said Nick dejectedly. "Thanks, Ezra."

Not knowing where else to go, he passed by the sheriff's office and walked back into the store. When he saw nobody was there, he called out, "Can I come upstairs?" Bear ran down the stairs to greet him. "Hiya, Bear." Nick patted him on the top of the head and walked upstairs.

"Do you want to stay for dinner, Nick? We have plenty." Mary Elizabeth grabbed another plate and looked at him.

"No, I just want to find Rachel. Ezra said she rented a horse and said she was going out of town. Mary Elizabeth, are you sure she didn't say anything else that might be a clue?"

Mary Elizabeth shook her head. "No, nothing else."

She sat in the chair across from Ryan. Looking up, she said, "Oh! *Jamie* said something, but I had no idea what it might mean or even if it means anything. He said, 'It was at the hotel—' and then Rachel pulled him out the door."

"*At the hotel?* What could that mean? I guess I'll walk on over to the hotel to see if anybody over there has a clue." Nick shook his head and looked at them, blinking to keep the tears away. "This makes me so sad. I was about to ask her to marry me. And now she's gone." And then he walked down the stairs and out the front door of the store.

As he was walking by the sheriff's office on his way to the hotel, he noticed movement inside. It was Josiah, so Nick backpedaled a few steps and walked into the office. Since he didn't really believe that anybody at the hotel could tell him anything relevant, a little delay didn't seem to matter. Besides, he felt compelled to walk inside and talk to Josiah.

"Hey, Nick. Why so glum?"

"It's Rachel. She's gone." Josiah sat at the desk, so Nick plopped into the chair beside him, still holding the teddy bear.

"What do you mean, gone? Where'd she go?"

Nick shrugged. "No one knows. She asked Mary Elizabeth to substitute for her, and that's all she would say. But Mary Elizabeth said that she was crying and seemed upset. The only clue is that Jamie said something like, 'It was at the hotel—' Not much to go on, but I'm headed over there now."

Josiah nodded his head, then seemed to think of something and looked at Nick, a shade of apprehension on his face. "I was at the hotel this morning. And while I

189

was talking, someone had come in and then abruptly left, before anyone saw who it was."

"Well, what were you saying?"

"Oh, tarnation, Nick, I hope this wasn't it." He looked down and wouldn't make eye contact with Nick. "I was talking about how you had said that you weren't the marrying kind, and that now you wanted to make it official. Everybody thought it was funny—sorry, Nick."

Nick gestured with his hand that it didn't matter. "I don't understand, though, Josiah. Why would that bother Rachel? Do you think that she didn't want to marry me, and she was trying to get away before I asked?"

Josiah shook his head without looking up. "No, Nick. The door slammed before she heard me say that now you wanted to make it official. If it *was* Rachel, all she heard was that you weren't the marrying kind. I'm sorry."

Nick, with the teddy bear on his lap, put his head in his hands. "Rachel thinks that I wouldn't marry her. And now I don't even know where she is so that I can explain. What am I going to do?"

"I'm so sorry, Nick. I'm so sorry." Josiah reached out and patted Nick on the shoulder.

Nick stood up. "I know what I have to do. I have to go find her. I'm a detective, right? I can do this. I can find her. Josiah, is it all right? I mean, can you cover for me tonight? I'm going right now."

"Sure, Nick, but it's almost dark. You can't go now."

"I have to, Josiah. I have to." Nick walked through his bedroom and out the back door of the office, and then he ran toward the livery. "Ezra! You here? Can you get me Cisco's saddle, please?"

By the time Nick reached Cisco's stall, the brushes

were already there, and Ezra was on his way to get the saddle. After a short warm-up, Cisco ran the rest of the way to the cave, walked through it, and ran most of the way to the ranch house. When Nick put him in the barn next to Snowman, the big speckled horse that Rachel had ridden in, he placed food and water in the stall, petted him, and then petted Snowman, too. "I guess you got her here safe, big guy. Thank you for that."

It was full dark by the time Nick walked out of the barn, and he saw that neither Madison's nor Zack's vehicles were there. Not wanting to go into the house, he climbed into the backseat of his pickup and lay down. All he could think about was how he could find Rachel. And when Madison and Zack didn't show up when it got late, Nick fell asleep, clutching the teddy bear to his chest.

CHAPTER FORTY-TWO

"YES, OF COURSE you can come! Both of you! Michael is here, and he'd love to see you! Come now!"

Rachel, having the answer that she wanted, smiled, and stepped back into the car. "We have a place to stay, Jamie. We're good."

"I want to go home, Mama."

"We'll talk about that later, Jamie." Now, all Rachel wanted to do was think about Michael. At one time, she thought she was going to marry him. Lindy had said he had a girlfriend now, but maybe that was over, too. What would it be like if it turned out that she married Michael after all? That would get her over Nick! Serve him right, too, the jerk. What Lindy said about Michael being in jail—that must be a mistake. The Michael she remembered was warm and sweet—well, until the time he slapped her.

She parked the car, leaned into the backseat to collect her things, and let Jamie out of the car. He took her hand without asking, and they walked to the front door. Before they even got there, the door opened, and Michael strode out to meet her.

"Rachel! So good to see you!" He picked her up and swung her around. Then he kissed her gently on the lips. "When Lindy said you were coming right over, I couldn't believe it! I heard that you had left town. Come on in."

He put his arm around her to escort her into the house, ignoring Jamie completely. She held out her hand, Jamie clasped it and followed her inside.

"I did, but I'm back now."

"To stay, I hope." Michael's eyes twinkled at her.

"Hi, Rachel!" Lindy ran across the room and hugged Rachel. "You look great!"

"Thanks, Lindy. And thanks for letting me and Jamie stay here for a while."

"How about if I take you out to dinner tonight, Rachel? Celebrate old times, you know? What do you think? Come on, say yes."

"Oh, Jamie has had a pretty hard day today."

"No, not *him*. I meant just you and me. Like old times."

"Oh, no, I—"

"Lindy will take care of him, won'tcha Lindy?" Michael put his arm around his sister.

"Sure, Rachel, no problem. He can play with Cody." She bent down to Jamie's level and put out her hand, "Hi! I'm Lindy. And Cody will be home from school soon, and you can play with him. Okay."

Jamie had his arms wrapped around Rachel's legs, but he said, "I'm Jamie. Okay."

"There! It's all settled. Let's go now! An early dinner." Nick put his arm out for Rachel to take. When Rachel hesitated, he said with a little sterner tone to his voice, "Come on! Lindy said she would take care of him. You trust her, don't you?"

193

Lindy nodded to Rachel that it was all right, so Rachel, reluctantly, knelt down to Jamie. "Jamie, you're going to stay with Lindy, and soon her son, Cody, will be home. He's the same age as you, and you two can play together, okay?"

Tears formed at the corners of his eyes, but he said, "Okay, Mama."

"Come on, Rachel!" Michael grabbed her roughly by the arm and pulled her toward the door.

Jamie ran up to him and said, "Don't you hurt my mama!"

"Shut up, kid." Michael put out his hand and gave Jamie a big push, so that he landed on his butt on the floor. He was too stunned even to cry.

When Rachel started to go to him, she noticed Lindy giving her a signal to just leave. And although she felt guilty, she thought that Lindy knew the best course of action. Michael scared her. A lot. Gone was his sweet and gentle side, and all that remained was the part of him that had caused him to slap her years ago. Going to dinner with him was the last thing that she wanted to do, but right now all she wanted to do was to protect Jamie. So she needed to get Michael away from him as fast as she could.

In the car, he insisted that she sit next to him, and in the restaurant—a place that they used to go to when they were dating, though the name had changed—he sat next to her, held her hand, and looked dreamily into her eyes. She didn't respond, but she didn't pull away, either. She was too afraid. And after dinner when he wanted to take her back to his apartment—for old times—she didn't know where she screwed up the courage, but she said no.

And when he tried to pull her close, she said,

"Michael, I'd rather wait until I'm more relaxed. I want to get back to Jamie. I'm sorry to disappoint you, but I need to get back to him. He really has had a hard day." Michael's eyes narrowed, but he allowed her to pull away. Then he said, "Tomorrow then. I'll pick you up, and you'll spend the night. Be ready." Then he reached across her and opened the door. "Go on, now. Go to your little brat. I'll get mine tomorrow."

CHAPTER FORTY-THREE

WHEN THE LIGHT woke Nick in the early morning, he stretched and found that he was stiff from sleeping in a cramped position all night. The teddy bear had fallen to the floor, but he didn't notice it and didn't remember it, either. He stepped out of the backseat of the truck and climbed into the front seat. Turning on the key, he realized that it was too early to go into the house. But he did look in the rearview mirror to see if Zack's and Madison's cars were there, and they were.

He turned the engine back off, and rested his head against the back of the seat. What could he have done differently to prevent this from happening? Nothing, he realized. He wasn't going to be mad at Josiah for what had happened—he could see how he and everybody else would think it was funny that he had said that he wasn't the marrying kind and then decided that he wanted to marry Rachel. Yeah, it was funny, but it would be funnier if she would actually marry him. Right then, with him sitting in the truck, alone, it all felt rather tragic. What if he never saw her again? What if she didn't listen to him? What if he couldn't even *find* her to explain? What would he do then?

Nick didn't know. And he didn't know if he even would return to the old Red Bluff to live anymore—if it wasn't with Rachel. He may have lived there alone for some time happily enough before he and Rachel got together, but now—no, he couldn't live there alone. It would be too sad for him to remember what he almost had—a family. And what about Jamie? He loved that kid. What if he never got to see him again, either? Maybe he could get joint custody or something, but that thought made Nick laugh. Yeah, right. Jamie wasn't even his kid, though it felt like he was his kid. It felt in his heart like it was his kid.

He supposed that he could get his job back on the force of the new Red Bluff. But even living here—in the town he had grown up in—didn't feel as much like home as the old Red Bluff. *That* was his home. And Rachel and Jamie were his family! He had to get them back. He just had to.

Closing his eyes for a minute, he somehow fell asleep, and was jarred awake by a sound behind him. Zack's truck! Zack's truck was backing out of the driveway! He had missed them. Jumping out of his truck, he tried to flag him down, but Zack was already driving down the street. The only good news was that he was alone, so he hoped that Madison would still be in the house. Nick ran his fingers through his hair and knocked on the front door.

Madison answered, said a quick, "Hi, Nick," left the door open, and walked away.

"Madison! Wait! I need to talk to you!"

"Come into the kitchen, then. I need to eat and leave. What's up?"

"Do you know where Rachel is?"

Madison shrugged. "No, don't have a clue."

"But what about the horse?"

"What horse?"

"You know, the big white speckled horse in the barn!"

"Oh, yeah. She left me a note to please take care of the horse, and she'd be in touch in a few days."

"That's all the note said?"

"Yup. That's all." She stuffed a piece of toast in her mouth and washed it down with some orange juice.

"Do you know where she lives, or where I might be able to find her?"

"I know she gave up her apartment when she moved back there. But that's all I know. Jenna might know. You could ask her."

"I need to find out now. It's really important, Madison. Really important." He tried to keep the tears from coming, but they slid down his face in big drops.

Madison stopped eating. "Oh. Okay. Someone called her here the other day. I think her name was Lindy."

"Do you have her last name or her number or anything?"

"I wrote Rachel a note and gave it to her. Let me go check Jenna's room. She called her from there." Madison rushed out of the room and came back shaking her head. "Sorry, Nick. She must have thrown it away."

Nick jumped up. "I'll go through the garbage!"

Madison shook her head again. "They picked it up yesterday."

"There has to be something, Madison. There has to be something." Nick looked around the room, but didn't see anything. "I know! You said you wrote her a note. Where did you write it?"

"On the pad in the living room, by the phone. Listen, Nick, I need to go get dressed. Good luck with it."

"Wait, Madison. Do you have a pencil?"

"Sure in Jenna's room. I'll get it, but then I need to get going." She walked off and walked back a second later with two pencils in her hand. "Here ya go."

Nick already had the pad of paper in his hand. He took it and the two pencils back into the kitchen. Gently rubbing the pencil over the pad of paper, pieces of words started appearing. But they weren't the ones he wanted to see. Standing up, he walked to the edge of the living room at the hallway. "Madison! Do you still have the note that Rachel left you—about the horse?"

"It's in the trash in the kitchen. That was after the garbage collection, so it should still be there."

Nick rummaged through the trash and was grateful that they had a garbage disposer, or the note might have had some egg or coffee grounds or worse on it. But he was lucky. There it was. Picking it up, he sat back down at the table comparing the words that had appeared with the note. There were numbers behind it, and he could almost make out the word Lindy.

"Any luck?" Madison appeared in the kitchen doorway.

"I've got a few numbers, but not enough yet. I'm still trying, though. Thanks for your help, Madison."

"I hope you find her, Nick. And you're welcome to use the phone after you figure out all the numbers. Good luck!" And Madison raced from the room and out the front door.

Fifteen minutes later, Nick had four numbers for sure. Of the remaining three, two numbers had only two possibilities—eights or fives or one of each—and one

number could be anything. He wrote down the four
definite numbers and the other possibilities and sat down
on the floor by the phone. He would have to try a lot of
numbers to figure out which one was right. But he was
willing to sit there all day if it meant finding Rachel. Ten
minutes passed with no luck. He had tried 0-9 with a
five, and then he started 0-9 with an eight. After two
phone calls, a woman answered. When he asked if
Rachel was there, she hesitated, and his heart leapt.

CHAPTER FORTY-FOUR

With her hand on the receiver, Lindy asked, "Hey, Rachel, it's Nick. Are you here?"

Rachel, surprised but clear-headed, said, "No. Tell him you haven't seen me."

Then, a blur. Jamie, who had been on the floor playing with Cody, who was kept home from school to keep Jamie company, ran to the phone and grabbed it out of Lindy's hands. He put it upside down on his face, but he screamed, "Yes! We're here! Come and get us, Nick! I miss you!"

Lindy took the phone from Jamie and said, "Look, I'm sorry, Nick. But Rachel told me to tell you that I haven't seen her. Now you know that I have, but she isn't interested. Good-bye."

Before Lindy had a chance to hang up the phone, Rachel, who had stood up and walked over, took it out of her hand. "Hello, Nick. I have nothing to say to you."

Lindy whispered in her ear, "Put it on speaker phone. I want to hear!"

Rachel pushed the button on the phone's base. "Rachel, it was all a misunderstanding. I know what you heard Josiah say, but you didn't hear all of it."

"What do you mean?"

"I mean, the next thing he said was, 'and now he wants to make it official with Rachel.'"

"What do you mean *make it official?*"

"I mean I want to marry you, Rachel! I want us to be a family! What a rotten way this has turned out. I wanted to ask you at the top of the Ferris wheel, but it didn't work out. And now I'm asking you on the phone! Geez!"

That made Rachel laugh, but she didn't say anything. Jamie stood at her side listening to every word.

"Well, Rachel? Yes or no? Will you marry me?"

Then it hit Rachel. He had asked her to marry him. She would have dropped the phone if she hadn't already put it down. But she took three steps and collapsed on the couch, crying. Lindy sat next to her with her arm around her.

"Rachel? You still there? Will you marry me or not? At least you could give me an answer."

Rachel said quietly to Jamie. "Jamie, tell him yes."

Jamie shouted into the phone, "Nick! Yes! She said yes! I told her that you loved us, but she didn't believe me! Yes, Nick! Yes! Can we go home now? Please."

While Rachel sat on the couch and wept, Lindy returned to the phone and gave Nick the address. "Tell him my car is here," said Rachel.

As Rachel gathered up their few belongings in the upstairs bedroom, she recalled the night before and how afraid she had been when she was with Michael. And how safe she always felt with Nick. She smiled to herself when she heard Jamie running around downstairs screaming, "We're going home! We're going home!"

After Michael had dropped her off the previous night,

202

she had run upstairs to apologize to Jamie for what Michael had done to him. And to explain why she hadn't defended him the night before—how men like that sometimes take it out on small children, just like Michael did when he pushed Jamie over. Jamie had said over and over, "He's a bad man, Mama, and Nick is a good man. Nick is a really good man." She had kissed him and spent the rest of the night holding Jamie close to her and stifling her cries in her pillow.

Now Rachel sat on the bed and thought how perfect everything had turned out. She hadn't mentioned to Lindy what had happened with Michael, or what he had said at the end of the evening, so Rachel had thought she would have to deal with the possible consequences by herself. And she had no idea what she was going to do about him. But now she didn't have to worry about it. She was going home—with Nick.

After picking up the big purse that held their clothes, she walked downstairs and dropped it to the side. The thought that crossed her mind was that she never had to see Michael again, and how grateful she was for that. Then the front door opened, and Michael stood there in the doorway, with his feet apart and his arms across his chest. Rachel just looked at him.

He pointed at her and narrowed his eyes. "I told you to be ready!" When she didn't respond, a smile crept across his lips. "Oh! You are ready, I see. You have your overnight bag. That's good, because you don't want to get me mad."

Rachel stood where she was, willing Nick to drive up before Michael carried her off with him. She knew he could force her, and she didn't think she nor Lindy could do anything about it. Then she heard the truck drive up, heard the door slam, and Nick came running in and stood behind Michael.

"Knock knock. Can I come in?"

Michael, surprised, stepped aside, and Nick walked straight up to Rachel and hugged her so tight that she didn't think he would ever let go. "I love you, Rachel."

"Who's this punk? Get away from *my* girl." Michael took a step toward Nick. He was taller than Nick, but slightly built, and Nick outweighed him.

Nick turned around and balled his fists. "*Your* girl? I don't think so, buddy."

"Nick! Nick!" Jamie ran up to Nick and wrapped his arms around his legs.

"Not now, little one. I'm a little busy."

"Nick, that man hurt me. He pushed me down. Hard."

"He hurt *you?*"

"What of it? He's a punk kid. He deserved it." Michael crossed his arms on his chest.

Nick took one step toward Michael and belted him right in the mouth. Michael fell to the ground. Nick stood over him. "He's not a punk kid. He's *my* kid. And don't get any idea about calling the police." Nick pulled his wallet out of his pants, opened it, and showed Michael his badge. "You touch him again, and I'll have you in jail for child abuse so fast that it will make your head spin." He reached out for Rachel. "Let's go."

Lindy and Cody had stood back during the confrontation. "Bye, Lindy. Bye, Cody," Rachel called out.

"Bye, Cody," said Jamie.

The three of them, Nick, Rachel, and Jamie, stepped over Michael's prone figure on the floor and walked to Nick's truck. "Gimme the keys to your car."

Rachel handed him the keys, and he opened the door of her car and stuck them under the visor on the driver's side. "I left a note for Zack and Madison. They'll pick it up later. Come on, let's get in the truck."

Nick lifted Jamie up, belted him into the backseat, and then gave Rachel his hand to help her in. As they were driving down the street, Jamie leaned over and picked up the stuffed bear from the floor. "Nick, what's this?"

"That's a teddy bear, buddy. It's for you."

Jamie hugged the bear to his chest. "Thank you, Nick. I knew you loved us."

"Not only do I love you, Jamie, but I'm marrying your mama. Which means from now on I'm going to be your papa! What do you think of that!"

Jamie leaned forward in the seat. "Mama, I promised not to unhook my seat belt. Can I now? Just so I can hug my new papa? Please?"

Nick winked at her affectionately and squeezed her hand. Rachel laughed and said, "Yes, Jamie, go ahead. Hug your papa."

CHAPTER FORTY-FIVE

NICK HAD BEEN so distraught over losing Rachel and so elated to get her back that he drove right past the street leading to the ranch. It wasn't until Rachel put her hand on his arm and said, "Where are we going, Nick?" that he realized where he was. But when Rachel looked at him, and their eyes met, he became so emotional that he had to pull the truck over. He unhooked his seat belt, leaned over, and kissed Rachel passionately on the lips.

"I love you so much, Rachel. I was so afraid that I had lost you forever. Please don't ever run away like that again. Just talk to me. I want you beside me always." He kissed her again. "I love you!"

From the backseat, Jamie yelled, "We love you, too, Nick! I mean Papa! We love you, too!" He bounced up and down on the seat.

Nick slid back over on the seat, put his hand on Rachel's cheek, and said, "How about we go out for a celebration dinner before we head back?"

Rachel nodded her head. "Sure!"

"Steak?" Nick asked.

"Steak, steak, steak!" answered Jamie from the back.

"Isn't it a little early for steak?"

"Steak, steak, steak!" Jamie repeated.

Nick and Rachel laughed, and Rachel said, "I guess it's settled then. Steak it is."

They drove to the Ore House restaurant and parked. Nick opened the door for Rachel and helped her out. Then he opened the back door and let Jamie out. Instead of having Jamie walk between them, Nick put his arm around Rachel, and Jamie held Nick's other hand. Nick held Rachel close to him, because he felt like he had almost lost her and now that he had her, he wasn't going to take a chance of her getting away again. He loved this woman so much—tears started coming to his eyes, but he blinked them away, turned to her, and kissed her cheek.

When they reached the door to the restaurant, he released her to open the door and let her and Jamie inside. They stood behind the sign that said "Please wait here to be seated."

A short time later they were brought to a corner table, which Nick was grateful for. He just wanted to focus on Rachel, and how wonderful she was, and that she was his. The time passed quickly, with Nick gazing into Rachel's eyes and thinking about how lucky he was, and Jamie bouncing up and down on the child's booster seat that they had given him. Then, dinner was over, and Nick paid the bill with his credit card.

As they walked outside toward the truck, Nick suddenly stopped, and his eyes shone. "I have an idea! How about dessert? Ice cream!"

Jamie jumped up and down and hugged Nick's knees. "You are the *best* papa!"

They walked two blocks down the street and two more

blocks over and arrived at the ice cream store that had more flavors than a person could even imagine. Jamie wanted to get a triple decker and started to pout when Rachel told him that it was too much. Nick said, "I have an idea! Let's all get the same size cone, so nobody feels bad about not having as much as someone else. We can all get our own flavors, but we'll get the same size. Is everyone agreed?" When Jamie saw Nick and Rachel both nod, he reluctantly nodded, too. "Okay," said Nick, "Rachel, do you want a triple decker?"

"Too much for me," Rachel said, shaking her head.

"Me, too," agreed Nick. "That okay, Jamie?"

"Okay," he said quietly.

Nick looked at Rachel while nodding his head, "How about a double decker?" he asked enthusiastically.

"Sounds great!" said Rachel, following along.

"I'd like that, too!" said Nick. "Jamie, is a double decker too much for you?"

Jamie jumped up and down. "No, it's perfect!"

A few minutes later, the three of them sat at a booth, Jamie's cone dripping down his hands, and Nick and Rachel eating a little more ice cream than they may have wanted, but enjoying it nonetheless. After they finished, Nick took Jamie in the bathroom to clean up, and they met outside. They walked back up the street, this time with Jamie in the middle again, all of them holding hands, until Nick stopped abruptly.

"Wait a minute! I want to go in here for a minute. I have a great idea!" Nick turned into the shop they were walking by and stepped in the door, followed by Rachel and Jamie. Nick walked toward the back, found what he wanted, paid for it, and showed it to Rachel and Jamie.

"It's for me!" cried Jamie. "My own sandle!"

"It's called a *saddle*, Jamie. *Saddle*," corrected Rachel.

"It's my very own saddle!" Jamie jumped up and down. "I want to carry it."

"Now, Jamie, this is a buddy saddle that hooks to the back of your mama's saddle, okay? You won't be riding the horse alone yet."

Disappointed, Jamie said, "Okay. But it's still *my* saddle, right?"

"Yes, Jamie, it's all yours."

The three of them walked up the street, Nick with one arm around Rachel on one side, and holding hands with Jamie on the other. They arrived at the truck, got in, and headed toward the ranch.

CHAPTER FORTY-SIX

RACHEL WATCHED AS Nick attached Jamie's buddy saddle to the saddle on the big, speckled horse. After Rachel climbed onto the big horse, Nick lifted Jamie into place. Jamie, in his enthusiasm, kicked his feet right into the horse's flanks. The horse didn't move.

"Jamie! Don't do that! See right here?" Nick pointed to the flanks. "Horses are sensitive there. You don't want to hurt him. Okay?"

"I won't do it again, Papa. I'm sorry." Jamie reached back and patted the horse above the tail.

Rachel stroked the horse's neck. "I think I like this guy." She put her face down into the horse's mane, and the horse nickered, turned his head, and looked at her. "I like you, Snowman! I think you're awesome!"

Nick handed Jamie his new teddy bear, smiled, and climbed onto Cisco's back. Then they all headed down the trail. Nick and Rachel had both been silent for the beginning of the trip, just occasionally looking at each other and smiling. But now, Nick asked, "Rachel, why were you over at your friend's house? Don't you have folks in town?"

"We went to her mother's and had to leave," said Jamie. "She was mean!"

Nick looked at Rachel and raised his eyebrows in question. "Really?"

Rachel nodded. "Yes, she's always been abusive to me, but"—she shrugged her shoulders—"I didn't think I had a choice—until I thought of Lindy. That's why we were there."

"Your mom's always been abusive?" Nick shook his head.

"Yeah. When I was in college, I went to therapy for it. She was a great counselor. When I told her how guilty I felt for not going to see my mother and then told her why I didn't go, she told me something that I've never forgotten. She said, 'Would you hang around a friend who treated you that badly? No, of course you wouldn't, because you care more about yourself than that. Why is family any different? There should be nothing sacred about family relationships if those relationships are wrought with pain. Your mother makes you feel bad about yourself? Fine. You're done. *Never* feel guilty about that again. You need to take care of yourself.'

"It took me awhile to let that sink in, and even longer to stop feeling guilty, but every time I returned to see my mother, it was the same old abuse, and I realized that the counselor was right. I cared about myself too much to put myself through that any longer.

"The only reason I went there yesterday is because I didn't know where else to go."

"I'm sorry about all that, Rachel. Really I am."

"No reason to feel sorry. I didn't hear it from you, and if I had stayed a few seconds longer, I would have been ecstatic."

211

Nick smiled. "So you're ecstatic about marrying me?"

"I'm essatic about you being my papa!" Jamie said.

"Yes, Nick, I am." She smiled at him. "I definitely am."

"Soon?"

"As soon as you want, I'm ready."

"Oh, good! I was hoping that you didn't want a long engagement. Where shall we do it? New or old Red Bluff?"

"How about both?"

"Both? Why?"

"Well, the old Red Bluff is our home now, but I told Lindy that I'd invite her to the wedding, and I'm not ready to have her go there yet."

They came to the cave, and Nick led the way. "What do you mean *yet*?"

"Lindy's ex-husband just got out of prison—for domestic violence. He hasn't contacted her yet, but she's afraid that he might. She wanted somewhere to go—just in case."

Nick moved uncomfortably at the information. "Gee, that's tough. Did he hit the kid, too?"

"I think so, yeah. And I found out that Michael—who had been my boyfriend—was also in jail for a while for domestic violence. He had slapped me when we were going together, and I always thought it was my fault."

"That's often what domestic violence victims think. 'If I only hadn't made him mad—,' but that's never true. Violence is never the answer." Nick shook his head and exhaled quickly. "I saw so much of that when I was on the force. It's never a good situation, and unfortunately, even after the violence, the woman usually takes the abuser back."

212

"I know. Lindy took Ray back a bunch of times until he put her in the hospital with broken bones. The guy's a monster. I hope he leaves Lindy alone, but honestly, I don't think he will. He's that kind of guy. I'm surprised that he hasn't contacted her yet."

"How long's he been out of prison?"

"Less than a month, I think."

"Maybe she'll get lucky, and he won't contact her."

"I hope so," said Rachel. "I really hope so."

The horses walked into the livery and toward the back. Cisco stopped in front of his stall. Nick swung off and pulled Jamie out of his new buddy saddle.

Rachel slid off Snowman and put her arms around the big neck. "You're awesome, big guy. Thank you for taking such good care of us."

"So I guess you liked him then, Rachel?" Ezra asked.

"He was wonderful, Ezra! Thank you so much!"

"Do you want me to take care of your horse, Nick?"

"Yes, please, Ezra, and"—Nick patted the speckled horse's rump—"keep this one separate, would you?"

"Sure thing, Nick. Sure thing."

CHAPTER FORTY-SEVEN

NICK AND RACHEL held hands, and Jamie held Nick's hand in both of his, jumping up and down all the way to Rachel's house screaming, "Papa! Papa! Papa!"

Jamie's antics made Nick and Rachel laugh, but they were more involved in staring into each other's eyes and smiling. When Rachel stumbled on a rock in the road, she grabbed Nick with her free hand and held on. "Nick, I love you so much. And so does Jamie. It was such a horrible two days thinking that you didn't care about us." She looked down.

"Rachel, I love you and Jamie more than I can say. You both are so important to me—more important than anything else in my life. I'd do *anything* for you." He stopped in the road and hugged Rachel and Jamie to him. "And those two days were horrible for me, too. I slept in my truck so I could catch Zack and Madison to see what they knew."

When they arrived at Rachel's house, Nick opened the door to let them in. Jamie grabbed Nick's hand and pulled him into his bedroom. "Let's play with the trains, Papa!" So Nick sat down on the floor with Jamie, as

214

Rachel sat on the bed and watched.

After a while, Nick stood up and stretched. "That's enough for today, Jamie. You can play by yourself now."

"Okay. Thank you for playing with me, Papa," Jamie said without looking up.

"You're welcome, little man." Nick ruffled Jamie's hair and then took Rachel's hand, pulled her into a standing position, and led her into the living room. "Let's sit down for a while." They sat on the couch, next to each other, with Nick's arm around Rachel, and Rachel's head on Nick's shoulder. "This feels good."

"Yes, it does. I was so afraid that I'd never see you again, and after what I heard—or thought I heard—I didn't want to." Rachel snuggled into him.

Nick kissed the top of her head. "Tell you what. Let's not talk about it anymore. It doesn't feel good to either of us, and I think it would be best to forget all about it. I love you, you love me, and we're getting married. That's all that matters now, right?"

"You're right, Nick, you're absolutely right."

"Mama! Papa! I'm hungry!" Jamie rushed into the room and plopped himself on Nick's lap.

"Hungry? Already? Didn't we just have steak and then ice cream?" asked Rachel moving over to give Jamie more room.

"I'm hungry! I'm hungry!" Jamie bounced on Nick's lap.

"Rachel, I'd be happy to cook something. Do you have anything in the house?"

"No, Nick. I usually get something from the store or if I'm too tired, I go to the hotel and get something to go."

"Oh, yeah, this is the nineteenth century. Maybe we could get a solar cooler like Ryan has." Nick pushed

Jamie off his lap and stood up. "But for now, how about I go to the store and get us something and then come back here and cook it?"

"Sure, if you want to. I can help," said Rachel.

"You can rest. Just keep me company—that's all the help I need. Are you planning to teach tomorrow? Mary Elizabeth will probably ask me."

"Yeah! No reason not to. I love my job. That's why— oh—I'll stop there."

Nick laughed and leaned over to kiss her on the lips. "I'll be back soon."

"Can I go with you, Papa? Please? Please?"

Nick picked Jamie up, swung him around, and put him back down. "Not this time, big fella. See ya soon!" He strode out the door, and taking care that Rachel wasn't in front of a side window, he walked back to the livery.

"Ezra? You still here?"

"Still here, Nick. What'cha need?" asked Ezra coming out from the back.

"I'd like to buy that big, speckled horse that Rachel rented. Oh, and I'll pay you for the rental, too."

"She liked young Snowman, huh? Sure, I'll sell him to you. I wouldn't want to disappoint Rachel. But, forget about the rental. Let's call it a test riding session."

"Oh, Ezra, you're the best! I see you have him down here with Shiloh and Cisco. Can he stay here so all the horses are together?"

"Sure, Nick, no problem. Did you want to open up the third stall so he can be with your other two?"

Nick stroked Cisco and Shiloh over the fence. "No, these two have always been together. I just didn't want to separate them. Snowman can stay on his own. He'll be

216

close enough." Nick reached for his wallet, then thought better, and put his hand in his pocket and pulled out some change. "How much do you want for him?"

Ezra put his hand under Snowman's chin and opened up his lips. Pointing to his teeth, he said, "He's still a young horse. Does fifteen dollars sound fair?"

"Fifteen dollars? For a horse?" Nick shook his head and blinked.

Ezra knotted his brow. "Well, you're a good customer, Nick. I guess, for you, I can sell him for twelve."

"Twelve dollars?" Nick laughed and counted the change in his hand. "How about twenty dollars, and we call it even?"

Ezra held out his hand, Nick put the change in, and Ezra counted it. "Twenty dollars. I thought you were kidding. That's too much for this horse. He doesn't have papers or anything."

"I have a feeling that he's going to be worth every penny, Ezra. Keep it." He reached out and closed Ezra's hand around the money. "Hey, I do have a question for you, though. Do you ever get in any ponies?"

"Pony?" asked Ezra.

"You know, like a Shetland pony."

"Oh, no, nothing like that. We get some small horses in sometimes—you know fourteen hands or so—but no Shetlands. Sorry, Nick. You looking for something for that boy of Rachel's?"

"He's my boy, now, too, Ezra! Rachel and I are getting married."

Ezra put out his hand to Nick. "Congratulations, Nick!"

"Thanks, Ezra. Hey, do you have a light wagon that I could pull by myself with a light load?"

"Like Ryan's?"

"No, it would have to be lighter than that," said Nick.

"Oh! Is this for moving those strange chairs that you have in a stall back there?" When Nick nodded in the affirmative, Ezra said, "I think I've got just the thing for you. Be right back."

A minute later, he pulled out a small cart with two barrels on it. "I use this to clean the stalls, but I won't be using it until tomorrow some time. Do you think this will work for you? You might have to make a couple trips, but it's easy to pull, even with a load."

"It looks perfect, Ezra."

"Great. Let me get these off here for you." Ezra lifted one barrel out and Nick the other.

"Thanks, Ezra. I'm shopping now and cooking supper tonight, but I'll be back later to get this." Nick walked out of the livery and up the street toward the store.

Still smiling about buying a good horse for Rachel, Nick knocked on the back door of the store and walked in. Ryan sat at his easel in the back painting a picture, and Nick heard Mary Elizabeth out front helping a customer.

Ryan looked up briefly when he walked in. "Hey, Nick! You've got a smile on your face—you must have found her!"

"Yup. Found her and she agreed to marry me!"

"So when is the big happening?"

"Sometime soon, but we didn't talk about when. I'm thinking something small, though. No big deal. I just want to get it done. I don't want to lose her again."

Mary Elizabeth walked in from the front of the store. "Did I hear that you're getting married, Nick? Congratulations! I'm glad it worked out. You two are perfect for each other."

"Thank you, Mary Elizabeth. And thanks for your help with everything."

"Oh, Nick," asked Ryan, "will it be here or *there*?"

"Both, but here first. Rachel has some friend that she doesn't want to bring here. But it will be brief there, too, is what I'm thinking." Nick walked toward Mary Elizabeth. "I need some stuff for dinner, Mary Elizabeth. Can you help me with that?"

"Yes, of course. What do you have in mind?"

"What do you have? Oh! And by the way, now that Rachel is back, she'll teach tomorrow. Thank you for filling in for her."

"No problem. It was fun—for one day. I wouldn't want to do it as a job. Of course that little boy, Oscar—he's a challenge, isn't he? He's the one that pushed Jamie in the street, right?"

Nick nodded. "Yeah."

Five minutes later, Nick walked out of the store with a whole chicken, several potatoes for mashed potatoes, some butter—because he wasn't sure if Rachel had any —fresh asparagus, and several items so he could make a salad. He smiled as he headed toward Rachel's house. Nick enjoyed cooking, and living at the sheriff's office didn't afford him that privilege. He'd been eating at the hotel for most meals. Now, he had the opportunity not only to cook, but to cook for *two* people that he loved. It was perfect.

CHAPTER FORTY-EIGHT

WHEN NICK LEFT, Jamie hanging onto his legs until he reached the door, Rachel sighed. Then Jamie went into his room to play with his train, and Rachel followed. She stood to the side of the window so she could look out, but no one could see her looking—because she wanted to watch Nick walk away without him knowing. The way that it had turned out was so perfect. He did love her and Jamie as much as they loved him, and he was going to marry her! Rachel felt like all her dreams were finally coming true.

Instead of walking up the street to the store, Nick cut back down the block toward the livery. Although she didn't know why, she figured that he wanted to check on his horses. He loved them so much and only wanted the best for them—and she had a feeling that's the way he felt about her and Jamie—only wanting the best for them. He was everything in a man that she had ever dreamed of. And now, he was all hers.

After he disappeared into the livery, Rachel walked out of Jamie's room and into her own. She hadn't had room for many clothes, and now she just wanted to change. Pulling on the jeans that she could only wear around the house because the people of the nineteenth century wouldn't understand about a woman wearing pants, she then put on a new blouse that Ryan had ordered for her. It was beautiful! *She* was beautiful! Nick made her feel beautiful, and what a wonderful feeling that was.

Later, when Nick walked in with his arms full and his eyes sparkling, Rachel almost started crying. But she held it back with a couple of long blinks, and she welcomed him back home. He placed all the groceries on the wooden counter, grabbed her into his arms, kissed her, and then smiled at her.

"I'm going to love cooking for you, two." Then he looked alarmed. "Unless you want to do all the cooking —"

She smiled warmly at him. "No, Nick. I've tasted your cooking. You're a much better cook than I am. I'm happy to let you do the cooking! He's handsome, affectionate, loyal—and he cooks! What a bonus!"

Nick laughed and turned back to the counter. As he began organizing the groceries, he asked, "Do you have a pan to put the chicken in?"

"Oh, we're having chicken? Awesome! Yeah, right here." Rachel handed him the pan. "Do you need anything else?"

"I think I know where everything else is from the last time. Just keep me company."

Rachel sat at the table, next to the kitchen, watching Nick prepare dinner. He lit the woodstove in half the time it usually took her to get it started, and by the time it was warm enough, Nick already had the chicken ready to go in. Then he put water in two other pans, one for the asparagus and one for the potatoes. After looking at his watch and noting the time, he sat down at the table with Rachel.

"Papa?" called Jamie from the bedroom. "Would you play with the barn animals with me, please?"

"Not now, sweetie, I'm sitting with your mama right now." Nick moved his chair closer to Rachel's and put his arm around her. "Remind me to put the water on for the potatoes and asparagus. And speaking of asparagus, when did you want to get married?"

The comment made Rachel laugh. "Well, speaking of asparagus, I'm ready anytime you are."

"Really? How about this weekend? I'll arrange for someone to marry us on Saturday—unless you want to get married in the new Red Bluff first."

"No, marriage in the new Red Bluff is for show—and most likely, just for Lindy. Maybe we could get married at city hall with Lindy and someone else for witnesses. That would work out."

"Sounds perfect. That way we'll have marriage licenses in both places—cover all the bases in case we ever want to live *there* again."

"Would you want to live there again?" Rachel looked at him, wondering what his response might be.

"No, not really. You?"

"No. I love it here."

"Good, then we're agreed! We'll get married this Saturday! Awesome!" Nick kissed her, then stood up and put a pan of water on the woodstove. While he waited for it to boil, he peeled the potatoes and started making the salad.

Soon they were eating Nick's delicious cooking, and just as fast, supper was finished. Nick stood up quickly and cleared the table. When Rachel stood up to help him, he gently pushed her down and said, "Let me take care of it tonight. Next time I'll let you help."

Rachel smiled at him and stayed seated as she watched him clean everything up. After he washed all the dishes, he walked with her into the living room and sat on the couch. They snuggled on the couch and kissed and talked for a while, until Jamie fell asleep on the floor at their feet, his new teddy bear grasped tightly in his arms.

"I'll help you put him to bed, and then I have to leave," whispered Nick.

"It's still early, Nick. Do you have to leave so soon?"

Nick nodded. "I'm exhausted. I slept in my car last night and didn't get much sleep." He picked Jamie up and carried him into the bedroom. While Rachel pulled the shirt off Jamie's head, Nick took the boy's shoes off. His pants came next, and after they tucked him in and put the teddy bear beside him, they both kissed him on the forehead and walked out of his room.

"Good-night, Rachel. I love you, and I'll see you to-morrow." He kissed her slowly and passionately.

"Good-night, Nick. I love you, too." She stood in the doorway and watched as he walked up the street toward the sheriff's office.

CHAPTER FORTY-NINE

NICK HAD FELT her eyes on him as he walked up the street even though he didn't turn around. He was too excited about what he was about to do, though he'd wait awhile until all her lights were out before he started. An hour and a half later, he walked out the front of the sheriff's office and down the street. When he walked by Rachel's house, all the lights were off. If there had been any light on, Nick would have returned to the office to wait. But now he strolled down the street with a sense of purpose and walked into the livery.

Ezra had left the cart in front of Shiloh and Cisco's stall and had even loaded it with four of the desks. Nick shook his head. Ezra was quite a guy. Putting his shoulder into it, he pulled the wagon out into the street and headed toward the schoolhouse. After pulling it up to the door, he hoped that the door would be unlocked. It was. In these times and in this town, not many people locked their doors—or had to.

Two by two, Nick carried out the old chairs from the classroom. He left them out in front, and then carried in the four chair-desks from the wagon, putting them in place as he went. After loading the twelve chairs onto the wagon, he pulled it back to the back of the livery. Then he unloaded the chairs, and loaded up four more of the chair-desks. Returning to the school, he set them up in the classroom, and then headed back to the livery for one more load. He placed the last four chair-desks onto the wagon and moved the twelve chairs that he had taken from the school into the stall. One more trip to the school and he was nearly finished. It was dark, and he didn't dare light a flashlight of any kind for fear that Rachel might get up and look out the window. But he looked at the shapes of the chair-desks that he had just arranged, and he smiled. That should please Rachel. Then he left the wagon back at the livery and walked back to the sheriffs office, where he slept soundly all night.

First thing next morning—he had checked the sign and knew they opened early—Nick quickly strode down to the telegraph office. After handing the man the note requesting a minister on Saturday and watching him click away to send the message off, Nick asked, "How long does it usually take to get a response?"

"If you wait a few minutes, it should be right up. The minister is the operator's brother."

Nick glanced out the window nervously, wanting to reach the schoolhouse before Rachel, so he could see her face when she saw the chair-desks. "Oh, I really need to leave. I'll stop by later."

"Suit yourself." The man shrugged his shoulders.

"Thanks." Nick walked out of the building, took two steps down the street, and the door opened behind him.

"Hey! I got a response to your request. The minister will arrive Friday by stage so he'll be here in plenty of time for the wedding on Saturday. He asks if you could please reserve a room for him at the hotel."

"Great! Thanks! I will!" Nick smiled and picked up his pace toward the schoolhouse. When he got even with Rachel's house, the door opened, and Rachel and Jamie walked out. "Good morning, beautiful!"

"Papa!" Jamie ran to Nick and hugged him.

"Hi, Nick. What are you doing around here so early?"

Nick kissed her. "I just arranged for the minister. He's coming Friday on the stage and will stay at the hotel for the night."

"Oh, Nick!" Rachel reached up and put her arms around his neck.

Nick put his arm through hers and walked them both across the street to the school. When he opened the door for them, Rachel walked in and immediately turned around to talk to Nick, so she didn't notice the chair-desks. It wasn't until Jamie shouted, "Mama!" that Rachel turned around and saw them.

At first, she just looked at them, and put her hand to her mouth, flabbergasted. Then she looked at Nick and noticed the big smile on his face. "Nick! You did this."

"Guilty."

"Oh, Nick." She wrapped her arms around him and kissed him. "Thank you so much. They're awesome!"

"You're welcome. I'm sure the kids will get a lot of use out of them."

Jamie was sitting in each seat in turn, moving his butt around in the chair and saying, "Comfortable, comfortable" every time he sat down.

Rachel and Nick saw what he was doing and laughed. "I have to run now, Rachel. Have a good day at school. I'll see you tonight—I'll cook again, if that's okay."

"Bye, Nick!"

"Bye, Papa!"

Nick walked out of the schoolhouse with his shoulders back and a smile on his face. After he made arrangements for the minister at the hotel, he was going to make a quick trip to the new Red Bluff to see if he could find a gentle pony for Jamie. That would please the little guy. Everything was just perfect. He thought about how awesome his life was, and that when he married Rachel, it was about to get a whole lot awesomer!

CHAPTER FIFTY

RACHEL STOOD LOOKING at the chair-desks. How thoughtful of Nick to do that! She felt grateful at how wonderful he was and how everything had turned out. As she walked to her desk at the front of the room, she put her hand on the desks as she passed them. They didn't look much like nineteenth-century desks, and she hoped that Josiah wouldn't throw a fit when he saw them. But they were so perfect, and she knew that her students would get a lot of good use out of them. Nick was so awesome.

Still looking out at the classroom and watching Jamie, who was still moving from chair to chair, although he wasn't wiggling his butt anymore, she realized how lucky she was to have someone like Nick in her life. Everything was good before he came into her life, and now—now everything was so wonderful that she couldn't believe it.

When it got later and kids started filing in, they immediately walked up to her desk. "Miss Jenkins, are you all right?" "We missed you yesterday." "Mrs. Leyton was nice, but we want _you_ to be our teacher." "We were worried about you, Miss Jenkins." Even Oscar had come up to her desk and said, "I'm glad you're back." She was overwhelmed at the students' response to her absence the day before.

After they finished talking to Rachel, the students noticed the new chair-desks, and a new round of conversation ensued. "What are these?" "Where are our old chairs?" "Wow, look, we don't need our laps, anymore!" Five minutes later, Rachel finally managed to get everyone seated and on task, and lessons began in earnest.

When lunchtime came, Rachel felt relieved. It had been an overwhelming few days, and she was looking forward to the end of the school day, when she could go home and relax and help Nick cook dinner. What an idyllic existence! She leaned back in her chair and closed her eyes. Not that many minutes passed, before she heard footsteps coming toward her.

Susie Morris strode right up to the desk. "Miss Jenkins, Oscar pushed Jamie down. Again!"

"Susie? What? What do you mean, again?"

Susie looked down. "Well, he's done it before, but Georgina, my best friend, didn't want me to tell you because she likes Oscar." She looked up and stuck out her chin. "But Georgina isn't talking to me today, so I decided that I would tell whether she likes it or not!"

"Thank you for telling me, Susie. I appreciate it. Would you mind telling the other kids that it's time to come in from dinner? Thank you."

"Yes, Ma'am." Susie skipped through the classroom and out the door.

More trouble with Oscar. Rachel shook her head. When was that kid going to straighten up? Maybe never would be the correct answer. And Jamie! Why hadn't he told her that Oscar was pushing him down? She needed to get him to be more assertive. She sighed. Now she had to talk to Oscar and tell him that if she caught him doing it again, she'd have to talk to his father. That was one thing that she dreaded doing. The father was a brute, and she didn't want to have anything to do with him. When she thought about it, she decided that she wouldn't talk to him at all. Threatening Oscar that she'd talk to his father was one thing, but actually talking to the father was not what she would do. There was always the chance—more than a chance probably—that he would beat Oscar again, and she didn't want to feel responsible for that.

The students started filing in and sitting down. When she glanced at Jamie as he sat down, he looked normal, not hurt at all. But he didn't say anything to her about Oscar. As they settled down, several of the students mentioned that they wanted a writing exercise so they could use their new desks some more. So she handed out paper and pencils and gave them an assignment. When they finished, they wanted another and another, and so the afternoon passed. At the end of the school day, as she was about to dismiss the class and call Oscar up to the front, the door opened and into the room burst Oscar's father with narrowed eyes and looking mean.

"Class dismissed," Rachel said. Jamie ran out the back with the other kids to play with the ones who dawdled before heading home. Oscar, curious, kept his seat in the second row without saying anything.

Rachel took a deep breath and looked at her desk so she wouldn't have to watch him walk toward her, so she didn't see Nick follow the big man inside. Then she stood up to face him, still not noticing Nick lingering at the back door.

"I heard you took in that Givens boy after his folks left town."

Rachel nodded. "I adopted him after his grandparents left town, yes." Where was he going with this, she wondered.

"Well, I ain't leaving, but as we was driving by today at dinnertime, we saw Oscar give the Givens boy a shove and push him down. So my woman and I talked about it this afternoon, and we want to get rid of the little no-account. He's too much trouble. He's been worthless since the day he was born, and I'm done with him." He pounded his fist on the desk. "So, you want him? 'Cause if you don't take him, I'm taking him over to the orphanage in the next town." He glared at Oscar. "I don't care what they do with him. They can hang him for all I care."

"Take him?" Rachel stammered. "No. I can't take him. He almost killed Jamie a week ago."

"Fine. I'll dump him off at the orphanage, then. All the same to me. We just want to be rid of him." He turned to walk out.

Then a voice from the back said, "*I'll* take him."

The voice sounded oddly familiar to Rachel, and she looked up. Stunned, she said, "Nick!"

As Oscar's father headed toward him, Nick said, "I'll take him." He put out his arm toward the boy. "Come here, Oscar."

"Fine. And I don't care what you do with him or to him. Just keep him away from me and mine. His bedroll is on the step." Oscar's father disappeared out the door.

"But, Nick—our plans." Rachel looked at Nick who had one arm around Oscar, and she couldn't believe it.

"Our plans just changed. Now we have *two* sons."

231

"But, but, *him*. He tried to hurt *Jamie*. And you *love* Jamie."

"Rachel, this is the right thing to do. You know what happens to kids in nineteenth-century orphanages. I can't let that happen to someone I know."

"But, Nick—"

"It's the right thing to do, Rachel. And I *have* to do the right thing."

Rachel clutched her chest over her heart and turned away. "Good-bye, Nick." Then she collapsed into her chair.

CHAPTER FIFTY-ONE

NICK THOUGHT HE had heard wrong when Rachel said "Good-bye," but when she turned away and started crying, he knew that he hadn't. He didn't say a word, just led Oscar out the door, and told him to pick up his bedroll. Then they headed down the street toward the livery. They started out with Nick's arm around the boy, until Oscar shoved it off. "I don't like that. Get your hand off me."

Nick knelt down beside the boy and put his hands on his shoulders. "Listen, Oscar. It doesn't matter to me what you like or don't like. You'll do what I say. You don't have many options right now."

"I'll run away! I don't have to stay with you."

"You're right. You don't. That's your choice. But I can promise you this. You do what I say, and you will have a good life with me. I will treat you fairly, and I will never beat you."

"How do I know that you're telling the truth?"

"You don't. It's time you learned to trust, Oscar. You can start with me." Nick stood up. "Now, come on." He put his hand back across Oscar's shoulders, and although

Oscar kept moving his shoulders trying to get it off, he didn't say anything, and he didn't pull away.

Walking into the livery, Nick walked toward the back. "Ezra!" He walked past Shiloh and Cisco's stall and past Snowman's stall, and stopped in front of the next stall, which held a pretty black and white pony. As he stood there, Nick breathed deeply and tried to keep his emotions in check.

Ezra walked up. "He is a pretty, little thing, Nick. Do you like him, Ja—? Oh, that's not Jamie."

"No, this is Oscar. Oscar, this is Ezra. He takes care of my horses, and he's good at it. You *will* be respectful to Ezra." Ezra held out his hand, and Oscar, reluctantly, shook it. "Ezra, the thing is, I'm not sure what's going on with me and Rachel right now. The wedding may be off. So, could you put the pony somewhere that neither she nor Jamie will see it? Oh, and if you see her, you can tell her that the speckled horse is hers."

Ezra nodded his head slowly. "Okay, Nick, whatever you say." He pulled a halter and rope from the gate, put it on the pony, and led him out of his stall. Nick didn't see where he led the pony, but it was somewhere that Jamie wouldn't see it, so that was good.

"These are my two horses, Oscar. The spotted one is Shiloh and the other one is Cisco."

"They're pretty."

"Go ahead and pet them. It's okay."

Oscar's eyes widened. "It's okay to pet your horses? Really?" When Nick nodded, Oscar added, "My father never let me touch his horses."

Nick winced, shook his head, kneeled down and took Oscar's shoulders again. "Look, Oscar, your father and I are completely different men. I'd bet that he and I do most things differently. You treat my horses right, and you're welcome to pet them anytime. Okay?"

"Okay." Oscar reached up and petted Shiloh with one hand and Cisco with the other.

When Cisco nickered at the boy, Nick said, "See, he likes you."

Oscar glanced at Nick, blinked his eyes twice, and continued petting the horses. Nick thought the poor kid might start to cry any minute, but he held it together.

"You know, Oscar, I have an idea." He turned the direction that Ezra had taken the pony. "Hey, Ezra! You still around?"

"Yup, what'cha need, Nick?"

"You mentioned the other day that you sometimes see small—say fourteen-hand—horses. If you see a gentle one, I'm interested. Oscar needs a horse to ride."

"I'll be on the lookout for ya, Nick."

"Thanks, Ezra. Let's go, Oscar."

They walked outside, Nick's arm around Oscar again. This time Oscar didn't try to shrug it off. Instead, he looked up at Nick as they walked. "You're buying me a horse? My *own* horse?"

"Yes. How can we ride together if you don't have your own horse?"

"Ride together? You and me?"

"Sure! Why? What's wrong with that?"

"It's just—well, nobody's ever been that nice to me before." Oscar looked at the ground as they walked.

"What about your mom? Was she mean to you like your dad?"

"No, not mean. She used to treat me really well, but when my dad saw it, he'd tell her how stupid she was for treating a no-account like me so nice. Eventually, she just ignored me—but at least she didn't beat me like he did."

"Okay, Oscar, that's all over now. He won't hurt you again. Here we are."

They walked into the back door of the sheriff's office, through Nick's bedroom, and out the other door to the front, where Josiah sat at the desk. As soon as Oscar saw Josiah, he backed up against the closed door behind him and glared at Nick. "You tricked me! You were just pretending to be nice so you could take me to jail again! I hate you!"

Josiah looked on with raised eyebrows. "What's *he* doing here?"

Without answering Josiah, Nick kneeled down again. "Look, Oscar. I don't want you to say that to me ever again. I did not trick you. The bedroom we just passed through? That's where I sleep. You can leave your bedroll in there for now. And this evening, you can sleep in an *open* cell on a comfortable cot, or you can sleep on the floor of my room. It's your choice."

"You didn't bring me here to put me in jail?"

"No, son, I did not. I work here and sleep here." He opened the door of the bedroom. "Go ahead, put your bedroll in there."

Oscar did as he was told, and when he returned, Nick put his hand on his back and moved him toward Josiah. "Josiah, this is Oscar. He is now my son. And since I'm going to treat him well, he is going to clean up his act from this point forward. Right, Oscar?"

"Clean what?" asked Oscar.

"Oh. You're going to start behaving. Right?"

"Yes, sir."

CHAPTER FIFTY-TWO

WITH HER HEAD down on her crossed arms, Rachel sat at her desk and sobbed, until Jamie came over and put his arm around her. "What's wrong, Mama? And why did Papa walk off with Oscar? Is Papa going to put him in jail for pushing me down—because it didn't really hurt."

Rachel sat up, wiped her eyes, and pulled Jamie close to her. "No, honey, Nick is not taking Oscar to jail. Nick has chosen Oscar over us. He's not your papa anymore."

Jamie broke away from her and stepped back. "No! He *is* my papa! Don't say that! He loves *me*!"

"Come on, Jamie. Let's go home."

"No! Not if you say he's not my papa! I don't want to go!" Jamie turned his back on her.

Rachel bit her lip and drew in a ragged breath. Never in the year that she had known him, had she ever had to raise her voice to Jamie, but she did now. "Jamie! We're going home! Now come on!"

Jamie, with tears streaming down his face, turned back and followed her out of the schoolhouse. When they came to the street, Rachel reached for his hand. At first he crossed his arms in front of his chest, but when she narrowed her eyes at him, he relented and gave her his fist to hold. As soon as they were across the street, he ripped his hand from her grasp. She was too distraught herself to say anything. After opening the door of the house, she walked straight to her bedroom and fell onto the bed in tears.

It wasn't until an hour later when Jamie came to the side of the bed and said, "I'm hungry, Mama," that Rachel sat up and wiped her tears away. She swung her legs over the side of the bed and motioned for Jamie to come to her.

"Come here, Jamie. I want to tell you how much I love you, regardless of what happens with Nick."

"I love you, Mama, but I love him, too."

"It's okay, Jamie. I love him, too, but we can't be a family as long as he has Oscar—that wretched kid."

"But, Mama, Oscar only needs love. That's why I never told you when he knocked me down—'cause he just needs love."

"Oh, honey, you're such a good boy." Rachel hugged Jamie to her.

"Let's go get something to eat, shall we? We'll pick it up at the restaurant and eat it here, okay?"

"Okay, Mama."

Before they left the house, Rachel washed her face and tried to look presentable. They walked out the door and up the street holding hands. Although Jamie kept craning his neck to look toward the sheriff's office, Rachel kept her gaze fixed on the hotel. She opened the door and felt relieved when no one but Granny was in there. In going there, she knew there was a chance that Nick and Oscar would be there, too.

"Hi, Granny," said Rachel.

"Hi, Granny," said Jamie.

"Hallo, you two! I suppose you've come for dinner, er supper. I still can't get that right!" Granny came out from behind the front desk.

"Yeah, I'll take two meals to go. We're not particular what it is."

"Why don't you stay here and eat? It'll do you good to get out for a while."

"No, Granny, I don't want to be here in case *he*," she motioned over her shoulder, "shows up."

"She means my papa, Nick, the deputy sheriff," said Jamie.

"Yeah, that's too bad, Rachel. I heard that the wedding is off." Granny raised her eyebrows. "But, you know, Nick was in here today, and he did not cancel the minister."

"He didn't?" That got Rachel's attention. "Is Oscar gone, then?"

"Come on. Talk to me while I get your dinner ready." Granny walked toward the restaurant's kitchen. "Oscar is the kid that pushed your little Jamie in front of the stage, right?"

"Yes, that's him."

"Well, the kid that was with him today was perfectly behaved."

"That will probably last one day," said Rachel, frowning.

Granny stopped getting the two dinners ready and looked at Rachel. "You know, Rachel, I've known Nick a long time. I've known Nick since he was a bad boy. He made a conscious decision back then always to do the right thing. And that's what he did today. You know that, don't you?" Granny went back to packaging the two dinners.

"Did Nick tell you to say that? Because that's exactly what he told me today, that it was the right thing to do."

"No, he didn't. That's my own observation. But you just reminded me. Nick asked me to tell you that he had already bought you that big, speckled horse that you liked. So he's yours."

"Nick bought me Snowman? Oh—" Rachel somehow stopped herself from getting emotionally swept away by Nick's kindness.

"Here's your two dinners. Pay me later, so they'll still be warm when you get home."

"Thanks, Granny." Rachel and Jamie turned to go out.

"One more thing before you go, Rachel. I've been in this world a long time now, you know, and I've learned a few things. And one thing that I've learned is that kids who need love the most are the ones who ask for it in the most unloving ways. Think about that. Bye."

Rachel didn't know why, but knowing that Snowman was all hers touched something inside her. When they got home, Jamie sat at the table ready to eat, but Rachel put the food down and started back toward the door. "Come on, Jamie. We need to go see Snowman."

"I'm hungry, Mama."

"Me, too. Let's go before we get any hungrier. We'll come right back." She grabbed his hand and whisked him out the door and down the street toward the livery.

Although she didn't know where Ezra kept him and she didn't want to call out to Ezra this late, she walked toward Nick's two horses, thinking maybe Snowman would be by them. And she was awarded with a nicker when she got close. Holding the big horse's head in her two hands, she kissed him on the nose. "You're all mine, Snowman, all mine. I don't know what to say. I'm overwhelmed with happiness. But we need to go home to eat now. We'll come see you tomorrow. Love you, Snowman." She kissed him again on the nose, took Jamie's hand, and they walked quickly back home so they could eat.

CHAPTER FIFTY-THREE

THAT EVENING, WHEN Nick and Oscar settled in for bed, Oscar having chosen to sleep on the floor of Nick's room instead of in the jail cell, Nick turned over and looked at the shape in the darkness. "You okay down there?"

"Sure. I'm used to sleeping on the floor. I just don't want to go in that cell again."

Nick leaned up on his elbow. "Listen, Oscar, I need to talk to you. I'm going to say this once, and I'll never say it again. If you ever try to hurt Jamie again, then we're done. And you better watch out for him, too, because if you're within fifteen feet of him when he does get hurt, then I'll blame you. Understand?"

"Yes, I swear it. I'll never hurt him again." Silence ensued for a couple of minutes, until Oscar cleared his throat. "You really love that kid, don't you?"

"Yes, Oscar, I really love him."

"Do you think that you'll ever love me like that?"

Without hesitation, Nick answered, "Yes, I do."

Nick heard an audible sigh and thought that was the end of the conversation. But after another minute, Oscar spoke.

"You kind of chose me over Miss Jenkins and Jamie. And you love him and were going to marry Miss Jenkins. And you're going to buy me a horse. I don't get it. I didn't even know that you *liked* me."

"I didn't choose you over them. I chose to do the right thing. And it wouldn't be right to let *anyone* go to a nineteenth-century orphanage. I couldn't let that happen. I didn't like you—especially after what you did to Jamie. But I like you a whole lot better now."

"Why?"

"You haven't done one bad thing since we left the schoolhouse—not that you could have with me watching you the whole time, but still. Oscar, truth is, you remind me of myself when I was young."

"You? You're a deputy sheriff!"

"I wasn't always a deputy sheriff. At one time I was a bad boy like you—probably worse. But I was fortunate enough to get arrested once, and I had to go to court—it changed everything for me. I met up with some compassionate people who understood me and believed in me, and they helped me. And *that* changed me. That's when I decided to become a cop—er, policeman."

"*You* were a bad boy? Really? You're not just saying that?"

Nick laughed. "No, I really was. See? It's hard to believe, isn't it? But people change, and I think you can change, Oscar. I believe in you."

"Nobody's ever believed in me my whole life."

"I figured that. Well, you can never say that again, Oscar, because *I* believe in you."

Oscar made a sound that might have been a cough, but probably wasn't. And his voice was very quiet when he said, "I won't let you down. I promise."

They both fell asleep then. Oscar slept through the night, but Nick woke up every couple of hours with the presence of another person heavy in the air. And he realized that if he and Rachel were going to work things out—and he believed they would—that he would have to get used to another person, or more like other people. He fell back to sleep thinking of Rachel and feeling like it would work out. Maybe not right away, but he knew that they would still get married, eventually.

When the morning light filtered through the half-closed door, Nick awoke and stretched. In a minute, Oscar looked around wide-eyed, then saw Nick and relaxed. "I didn't know where I was."

Nick smiled warmly at the boy. "You're here with me. Safe. No one will ever beat you again."

The boy pushed himself up on one arm and looked at Nick. "What if I do something really bad—I mean that doesn't involve Jamie—but what if it was really bad? Would you beat me then?"

Nick shook his head. "I don't believe in beating children, Oscar. So, no, I would not beat you." He swung his legs over the side of the bed. "C'mon, we have some time before you have to go to school. I want to work on something, and I want you to help me."

"I still have to go to school? Miss Jenkins is going to hate me for taking you away from her."

"No, she won't hate you. One thing I know about Rachel is that she's fair. She didn't even hate you after what you did to Jamie. She didn't like it, but she didn't hate you. Come on, let's get going."

Fifteen minutes later, they were both outside behind the sheriff's office, Nick sawing the wood, and Oscar hammering the nails in place. Nick had just remembered promising Rachel that he'd make her a composting toilet, and whether they got back together or not, he would keep his word.

"You're really good at that, Oscar!"

Oscar smiled, and Nick thought it was the first time that he had seen him smile. "Thank you."

When they finished, Oscar looked at Nick. "Are we going to carry it over to her house now?"

"No. Let's wait until she goes to school. Then we'll take it over. It shouldn't be too much longer."

"What's this for, anyway?"

"You use this instead of a necessary."

"Why? What's wrong with the necessary?"

"Nothing, but this goes inside."

"You mean you keep it inside *the house*?"

"Yup. Maybe she'll let you try it sometime. C'mon. How 'bout if you wait out front until you see her walk by down there?" They entered the back door of the sheriff's office, and before they emerged from the bedroom, Josiah walked in.

"Hey, you two. I see your boy is still here." He looked at Oscar. "I thought maybe you'd run away when you got half a chance."

"No, sir." He looked up at Nick admiringly. "I'm going to be a copper just like him."

"A copper?" asked Nick.

"A cop. Copper. Policeman. That's what you meant, right?"

"Yes, Oscar, that's what I meant." He glanced at Josiah and half whispered, "They have cops *here*?"

"Yes, Nick," Josiah said in a stern voice. "They have cops *here*."

Nick laughed at Josiah's response. "Okay, well, so they

do. Josiah, did you happen to see Rachel before you came in?"

"She and Jamie were crossing the street heading to the school." Josiah sat down at the desk.

"Perfect! C'mon, Oscar, let's carry that thing over there now so you can get to school on time." Then Nick looked at Josiah. "C'mon, Josiah, you can help, too."

CHAPTER FIFTY-FOUR

RACHEL HAD CRIED herself to sleep the previous night, and woke up in the morning with sticky eyes and an aching heart. She still felt angry with Nick about choosing Oscar over her and Jamie—even if he was only trying to do the right thing. At the same time, she appreciated that he had not only bought her the horse, but had given it to her after their "break-up." That is, if it was a break-up. She still wasn't sure. Another thought that had crossed her mind was what Granny said about kids who needed love the most. Oscar was certainly not loved where he had come from, not with that brute of a father of his. Heaving a deep sigh, Rachel stretched and crawled out of bed.

They had a quick breakfast, and Rachel got them both ready for school. Then they walked across the street, hand in hand. Jamie had wanted to bring his teddy bear to school with him—because he missed his papa, and the bear reminded him—but Rachel had managed to talk him out of it. Now, she opened the door of the schoolhouse and was accosted by the sight of another of Nick's generosities—the chair-desks. Pursing her lips together and closing her eyes, she made a mental note not to let these things get to her.

When the kids started filing into the room, and she looked up to see Oscar come in, she tried not to react. She had always been firm but fair to him, and that would continue. Oscar didn't make eye contact with her. He probably felt self-conscious over what had happened. Or perhaps he didn't have a clue what impact Nick offering to take him had on everyone else. Well, that wasn't even right. Everyone else only consisted of her and Jamie. There was nobody else affected. And with the environment that Oscar had come from, she couldn't blame him for willingly going with Nick.

Shaking her head to clear all thoughts of Nick, she began class and stayed busy enough through the morning to only occasionally have to push thoughts of him aside. When dinner time came, she sank back into her chair and dismissed the class. She put her head in her hands while she considered the possibilities. Although, she hadn't gotten far when she heard a commotion outside.

As she ran outside, her first thought was, "What has that rotten little Oscar done now?" Coming through the door, she saw Jamie lying prone on the ground, holding himself up with his elbows, and Oscar standing there shaking his fist and about to throw a punch. Was he going to hit Jamie while he was down?

"Oscar! What are you doing? You knocked Jamie down again? What is *wrong* with you?"

Oscar looked up surprised. "No," he said. "I didn't knock Jamie down."

"Yeah, right. Follow me right now, young man!" Rachel marched into the classroom, and when she glanced back, she saw that he followed reluctantly behind, with his head hanging. "Sit down right here while I get some paper and pencil. You're going to write 'I will never push Jamie down again' until your hand falls off!"

Oscar looked up, ready to cry. "But I didn't do it, Miss Jenkins. I swear I didn't."

"You expect me to believe that, Oscar? You *always* do it."

"Not this time. Really. I didn't do it. I was—"

"Mama! Mama!" cried Jamie from the door. "Reuben pushed me down hard! Harder than Oscar ever did! Don't punish Oscar!"

Rachel looked at him and put her hands on his shoulders. "It's okay, Jamie. I understand why you're doing this, and you don't have to defend him."

"I'm not, Mama. Reuben did it. Ask him." Jamie looked up at her with his eyes pleading.

While all this was going on, Oscar sat at the desk not saying a word and writing what Rachel had told him to write. Jamie ran back outside, and a minute later pulled Reuben into the classroom. Rachel, thinking that she had the correct culprit, had returned to her desk, seething that Oscar would do something like that. But Jamie pulled Reuben up to her desk. "Ask him, Mama, ask him."

"Oh, Jamie, you're getting carried away with this. Go outside and eat your lunch. Take Reuben with you."

"Mama! Stop it! Ask Reuben now! Please!" Jamie pulled at her hand until she looked up.

"Okay, but I already know the answer, Jamie. I know who did this."

"Ask him!"

"Reuben"—Rachel tilted her head and said it slowly

like she was forced to do it—"Did you push Jamie down?"

"Yes, Ma'am, I did," said Reuben.

Rachel nodded her head until she realized what she had just heard. "What? What did you say?"

"Yes, I pushed Jamie down."

"See, Mama? I told you he did it. Oscar was trying to protect me."

"Reuben, go to the back of the room, and do what Oscar was doing. Oscar, please give Reuben your paper and pencil and then come up here to my desk."

"Yes, Ma'am." Oscar walked slowly up to the desk with his head down.

"I'm so sorry, Oscar. I thought you had done it." She shook her head and reached out and touched his hand. "I'm so sorry. But why was your hand in a fist? When I saw that, I thought that you were going to hit Jamie."

Oscar looked down again. "No, Ma'am. I was about to give Reuben a sockdologer for hurting Jamie."

"Okay, Oscar. I'm sorry I accused you. You can go outside and enjoy the rest of your dinner time. Go ahead now."

Oscar nodded, kept his head down, and walked toward the door. Before he exited, he turned around and said softly, "Sometimes even bad boys can change."

Rachel sat at her desk chastising herself. She didn't exactly believe that Oscar had changed. It was probably like Reuben had beaten him to it, and Oscar would probably have pushed Jamie down later. But she had accused him unjustly, and that was bad. And she would make sure that it didn't happen again. Assuming is never a good thing, and that is exactly what she had done. Circumstantial evidence. Oscar standing over the scene of the crime with his hand in a fist. What else could she have thought?

The rest of the school day sped by, and after she dismissed the class, she and Jamie hurried across the street. She still felt an odd unease about what had happened with Oscar, and she knew what would make her feel more centered and more at ease: spending time with the big, speckled horse. Jamie insisted on bringing his teddy bear, and this time she couldn't talk him out of it. They walked over to the livery.

CHAPTER FIFTY-FIVE

NICK SAT IN the chair next to Josiah, and they were talking when Oscar walked in with his head down. He walked past Josiah, stopped in front of Nick and without looking up, said, "I have to talk to you. Can we go in the back?"

"Sure, Oscar, what's wrong?" asked Nick, concerned.

"Not here," was all he said. Then he opened the door to Nick's room, walked through it, and out the back door.

Nick followed and closed the door behind him. "Okay, Oscar, what's wrong? What happened in school today that you're upset about?"

Oscar looked at the ground. "I let you down. I'm sorry. You can go ahead and beat me now."

"Beat you? I told you that I wouldn't beat you. Tell me what happened."

"Jamie," was all Oscar could say.

Nick grabbed Oscar by the shoulders. "You hurt Jamie again?" he asked in a rough voice.

Oscar looked up then and said quickly, "No. No. I didn't hurt Jamie. But I didn't protect him, either. I didn't have time. Reuben pushed him to the ground before I could get there."

Nick relaxed once he heard that Oscar hadn't hurt him. "Okay, what did you do then?"

"I was about to give Reuben a big sockdologer for hurting Jamie when Miss Jenkins came out and saw us." Oscar showed Nick his fist.

"Go on."

Oscar shrugged. "Miss Jenkins thought that I had pushed Jamie down—'cause I had done it so many times before—and she brought me inside and told me to write 'I will never push Jamie down again' until my hand fell off. Then Jamie came in and said that Reuben did it and not me, but Miss Jenkins didn't believe him. She thought he was trying to defend me."

"That's interesting," said Nick. "Go on."

"Then Jamie went out and pulled Reuben in and made Miss Jenkins ask him. See, Reuben will always tell the truth if you ask him, but he won't volunteer anything. That's just how Reuben is. So Jamie finally got Miss Jenkins to ask him, and Reuben told her the truth. So she apologized to me and made Reuben sit there and write about not pushing Jamie down."

"You did fine, Oscar. I'm not mad at you."

"But you told me that I had to watch out for Jamie, and I didn't get there quick enough. I let you down." Tears started coming into his eyes, and he wiped them off his face, sniffled, and made himself stop crying.

Nick quickly grabbed him into his arms and hugged him. "No, Oscar, you didn't let me down. You did fine. You were protecting Jamie—even if you weren't quick enough. You did good. You did exactly what I would have wanted you to do—except maybe the sockdologer —you could have left that out." Nick laughed and kissed the boy's head. "You did great, Oscar. I'm proud of you."

Oscar pulled away from Nick and looked at him, big drops rolling down his cheeks. "You're *proud* of me? Nobody's ever said that to me before."

"Well, I have a feeling that you're going to be hearing that a lot from now on, Oscar. Come on, let's go see the horses. That always makes me feel better. Maybe it will work for you, too."

Nick put his arm around the boy and turned him toward the livery. They walked in together, and immediately Nick noticed Jamie playing with his teddy bear in front of Snowman's stall. Jamie didn't notice him immediately, but when he did, he ran into his arms. "Papa! Papa!" Nick picked him up and twirled him around. "How's my boy?"

"I miss you, Papa. When are you going to come over and make us supper again?"

Nick glanced over at the next stall and saw Rachel's back to him. She was busy brushing the horse and was ignoring Nick. "I don't know if that's going to happen, buddy. But I'll still see you in town."

"Okay," said Jamie sadly. He turned away, walked in front of Snowman's stall, and began tossing the teddy bear up in the air and catching it.

Nick opened the gate to Shiloh and Cisco's stall, walked inside, and closed the gate behind him. Oscar stood on the rails outside petting both horses. It happened so fast that Nick barely saw it. Jamie, in throwing the teddy bear up in the air, had wandered in front of the stall where Nick was. He threw it up and missed when it came down. The teddy bear landed in the middle aisleway. Jamie took a couple of steps to retrieve it.

254

Just then, a loud and sharp whinny came from the front of the livery. Suddenly, an out of control horse and rider came running down the aisleway toward Jamie, who had looked up and stood frozen when he saw the horse running toward him. Before Nick could even scream, Oscar had jumped down from the rail and pulled Jamie out of the way—the runaway horse just missing the both of them.

The two boys lay in the dirt, both of them scared. Oscar stood up first, and put down his hand to help Jamie up. Jamie said quietly, "Thank you for saving me, Oscar." He picked up his dusty teddy bear, stuck his thumb in his mouth, and walked to the front of Snowman's stall without saying another word.

"You're welcome." Oscar walked back to where Nick was.

Nick had glanced at Rachel immediately after the incident, but she had been kneeling down, brushing the horse's legs, and didn't see what had happened. Now, Nick came out of the stall, closed and latched it behind him, picked Oscar up in a big hug, and swung him around. Then he started walking toward the front of the livery, still carrying the boy in his arms. "Oscar, you are *awesome*! I am so proud of you! You are my *hero*! I bet nobody ever told you *that* before, either!"

"No, but could you put me down. I'm too big for this."

Nick laughed and put the boy on the ground. "Yes, I guess you are." He put his arm around Oscar and walked back toward the sheriff's office.

CHAPTER FIFTY-SIX

ALTHOUGH RACHEL HAD heard the whinny and the horse going by, she had watched Jamie earlier walk toward Nick's horses' stall, so she knew that he would be safe. And now, look at him, standing by the rails of Snowman's stall, holding his teddy bear—who looked a bit dusty—to his chest and sucking his thumb. Sucking his thumb? "Jamie! I've never seen you suck your thumb before! What's going on?"

Jamie took his thumb out of his mouth, looked at it like he didn't know what it was doing there, wiped it on his pants, and shrugged. "Can we go home now, Mama?"

"Sure, little one." Rachel stood on her tiptoes and kissed Snowman's face.

Before Rachel had a chance to open the stall door, Ezra walked by leading a prancing horse, with a bedraggled man following. Rachel heard Ezra say, "Don't tell me you want a spirited horse if you don't know how to ride a spirited horse! Someone could have gotten hurt!" She didn't hear the man's muffled response. She stepped out the stall door, latched it behind her, and held out her hand for Jamie.

He held on tightly and pressed against her, still clutching the dusty teddy bear in his arms. Rachel looked down at him curiously, but shrugged, and walked on. She thought he was probably upset at seeing Nick, as she was. And she was grateful that she had been able to hide her head while brushing the horse so she didn't have to look at him. She should have at least told him thank-you for giving her the horse, but at the time she was afraid that if she spoke at all she would break down. Later, she thought, she could send him a thank-you note.

When they walked into the house, Jamie ran to the back to use the necessary while Rachel looked around the kitchen wondering what they could have for supper. A few minutes later, Jamie came running in to her. "Mama! Mama! There is something funny back here."

"In the necessary?" Rachel asked.

"No, in the house." He grabbed her hand and pulled her toward the back of the house. "Where did it come from, Mama?"

Just inside the back door, stood a just-built composting toilet. Rachel shook her head. Nick built this for her and brought it over even after she had broken up with him. She sighed and knitted her brows. What a good guy.

"Where did it come from, Mama?" Jamie repeated.

"Oh, Jamie. Nick built it for us."

"Papa?"

She didn't have the energy to argue, so she nodded. "Yes," she answered and then walked into the living room and sank down on the couch. Jamie came in and sat on her lap.

"My papa is a really good man, Mama."

"I know, Jamie."

"And Oscar isn't as bad as you think he is, Mama. I thought you'd forgive him after he saved me."

Rachel was thinking of Nick and was only half listening to Jamie. "Saved you? You mean from Reuben this afternoon?"

"No, Mama, not then. From the horse!"

That caught Rachel's attention. "What horse? When? What are you talking about?"

"The horse that ran by and almost stepped on me— you know, at the livery."

Rachel had been holding him against her, but when he said this, she pushed him away so she could look into his eyes. "At the livery? I don't know what you mean."

"That horse ran by and Oscar jumped out and pulled me to the side. It was like what Papa did with the stagecoach, but there were more horses with the stagecoach, so Papa was braver."

"Oscar pulled you to the side when a horse ran by? Why didn't I see that?"

"I think maybe because you were petting Snowman. It's okay that you didn't see it, Mama. I already thanked Oscar for saving me."

Overwhelmed with emotion, Rachel nodded absent-mindedly and pulled Jamie close to her. "That's why you were sucking your thumb—" She put her face into the back of Jamie's head and said, "Oh, what a fool I've been! Let's go!"

Holding hands, Rachel and Jamie raced up the street to the sheriff's office. After stepping through the doorway, Jamie broke away from her and threw himself on Josiah. "Sheriff Josiah!"

"Hey, big guy! Hey, Rachel." Josiah stroked Jamie's hair. "I heard you had a close call today."

"Yup. Oscar saved me."

"Oh, he's a regular hero, is he?" asked Josiah.

"Yup! He's my hero!"

"Josiah, is Nick around?"

"Yeah, he and the boy are in the back. Go ahead. You can go through his room. I'm sure that would be fine with him."

"Come on, Jamie." Rachel held out her hand, and Jamie slid off Josiah's lap and grabbed her hand.

Rachel, feeling nervous but determined, took a deep breath, and then opened the door, walked through the room and out the back door. They didn't see her at first —they were cleaning up what was probably the scraps from making her composting toilet—but they seemed to be enjoying themselves, talking and laughing. Oscar looked like a different kid. And when she thought about it, she didn't think she had ever seen him smile or heard him laugh.

She let go of Jamie's hand and stepped forward. Oscar saw her first and glanced at Nick. Neither of them moved. Then Rachel headed straight for Oscar and threw her arms around him. "Thank you for saving Jamie, Oscar. I apologize for thinking that you couldn't change."

When Rachel released him, Jamie ran over and grabbed Oscar. "You're my hero! You're my hero!"

Rachel then turned toward Nick and slowly approached him. "I'm so sorry, Nick. I'm so sorry for doubting you." She looked at him uneasily, ready to cry if he rejected her, but feeling that she deserved just that.

Nick opened his arms, Rachel fell into them, and he gave her a long kiss on the mouth. "I love you so much, and I was hoping that you would change your mind."

As Rachel gazed happily into Nick's eyes, Jamie continued to chant, "You're my hero!"

Nick put his arm around Rachel, and they turned to face the two boys. "He's not only your hero, Jamie. He's your brother!"

CHAPTER FIFTY-SEVEN

THE NEXT TWO days passed blissfully away, with Nick cooking dinner for the four of them while the two boys played happily together. Oscar smiled and was polite, and Jamie was delighted to have a playmate. Rachel looked stunning as usual, and Nick could hardly wait until the wedding the following day.

The four of them went out to meet the stagecoach that was bringing the minister. It was late, needing some repairs at the last town, so it was after school when it arrived. There wasn't all the ceremony from their first arrival, but there were still plenty of people in town to watch its arrival.

Six horses pulling the stagecoach stopped in front of the hotel again, and the man driving the stage threw down a pouch of mail to Edward, who waited in front of the hotel. He gave it to Granny to go through before they brought it to the post office. The hotel received more mail than anyone else in town, so it was always dropped off there first.

As Nick and Rachel held hands and waited impatiently for the passengers to disembark, the two boys stood by the horses and petted them. The stage door opened, and Nick and Rachel were smiling and anticipating the minister's arrival.

An older man stepped down first, and he immediately turned and helped the older woman behind them. It wasn't until they stepped toward them that Rachel said, "Oh! It's you."

Nick didn't recognize the people, but Rachel had clasped his hand tighter at the moment of recognition. And then she stepped back when they approached her.

"Hallo, Miss Jenkins," said the man. "We wanted to thank you for taking care of Jamie, but now we've come to take him back with us."

"But you didn't even say good-bye to him. You asked me to give him away as if he was a puppy. No. You can't have him." Rachel said. Nick could feel her hand trembling in his, but she still stood up to them.

"He's our boy, and we want him back. My wife," he motioned toward the silent woman beside him, "can't stand to be away from him any longer."

At that moment, Jamie had caught sight of them and ran up to them. "Grammy, Grampie! You came home!" He was hugging them and kissing them. The woman was crying.

"See?" the man said. "He missed us, too. We're taking him."

"Taking me where?" asked Jamie, looking up.

"Taking you back with us to see your great-grandparents."

Jamie looked from Nick to Rachel. "But when can I come *home*?"

"Your home will be with us again, Jamie. Just like it used to be."

Jamie's eyes started filling with tears, and he ran to Nick and Rachel, holding them both. "What about my mama and papa?" he asked without looking at his grandparents.

"Your mama and papa? Jamie, you know they're gone. *We're* going to take care of you now, just like before."

"No! *This* is my mama and papa! I want to stay with them."

"You'll feel better when you get home with us," said the man, reaching out to pull Jamie away from his grasp of Nick and Rachel.

Oscar, who had watched the scene in silence, took two steps forward and came between Jamie and the old couple. "You're not taking him. He's my brother, and I won't let him go."

"Brother? What do you mean, brother? And what's this about Mama and Papa? What's going on?"

"I'm marrying Nick. Jamie has been calling us Mama and Papa since you left him behind. We have also adopted Oscar, who is now his brother."

"See here, young woman—" the man began, but was interrupted by his wife.

"They're a family." She shook her head. "Jamie has a family here. He's not alone. That's all I care about. Leave these good people alone, dear." Taking the man's arm, she pulled him away. "Come on, let's leave them in peace. They're good people."

They started walking toward the hotel. "You are welcome to come to our wedding tomorrow," called Rachel. As soon as they were in the hotel, Rachel collapsed into Nick's arms. "I thought we were going to lose him, Nick. I was so afraid that we were going to lose him."

"No, you weren't going to lose me. Oscar wouldn't let

them take me!" said Jamie, pulling Oscar toward Nick and Rachel in a group hug.

Granny waved to them from across the street. She skipped across the street carrying a letter. "Eliza and Samuel are coming home! They found Brian! And his children! Woo hoo!" Then she disappeared into the saloon to share the news there.

Her antics made Nick and Rachel laugh. "I didn't know Eliza very well before they left. Do you know what's going on?" Nick asked.

"Apparently, Eliza and Samuel thought that Brian was killed in the Civil War—like their other son was. But then Jenna found on the internet that he was still alive, so they went looking for him. Finding children with him is a surprise, though."

"More reason to celebrate, then." Nick kissed her on the top of the head.

"Isn't this cozy?" asked a voice walking toward them from up the street. "A regular family affair. Well, I've come to break it up."

Nick looked up and saw Oscar's father approaching them. "What are you talking about?"

"I have some work to be done. *He* can help. I guess he's not completely worthless, and I need him. You can have him back when I'm finished." The man stood with his arms crossed looking at Nick and expecting submission. Nick thought that most people bowed down to his false authority. Noticing how big around the man's arms were, he understood why.

Before Nick could answer, Oscar started to step forward to go with his father, but Jamie jumped in between them. "You can't take him. He's my brother, and I won't let him go!" Jamie stood there with *his* arms crossed looking up at the man with defiance.

"Why you little—" he raised his arm to strike Jamie, and Nick jumped forward grabbing his arm. Although the man outweighed him and was stronger, it didn't worry Nick. Oscar's father hadn't gone through the rigorous police training that Nick had.

"You touch my boy, and I'll kill you," said Nick, narrowing his eyes.

The man pulled away from Nick and raised his arm to strike him, but Josiah, who had appeared out of nowhere, caught his arm from behind. "I don't think you want to be hitting my deputy." Oscar's father backed away from Josiah's grasp and glared at him. "In fact, if you ever, I mean ever, bother these kind people again, I'll run you out of town like the no-account that you are."

"That's *my* boy, and I want him back!"

"I know how you treated that boy—and you don't deserve him back. As sheriff of this town, I am permanently and officially pronouncing him the son of Nicholas and Rachel Gallanti, and as such"—Josiah put his hand on Oscar's head—"he will from this day forward be known as Oscar Gallanti. Which means, tough guy"—he gave the man a little shove—"that he no longer belongs to you. You have *no* rights to him." Josiah stopped and put his hand on his chin. "Oh, one more thing to make sure we have everything covered. Oscar, would you like to go with *him*"—he pointed to Oscar's father—"or stay with *them*?"—he indicated Nick and Rachel.

Oscar wrapped one arm around Nick's legs. "*Them*," he said quietly.

"Then I guess it's settled. You can now go back to the rock that you crawled out from under. Now get out of here, before I kick you out of town, permanently." Josiah pointed out of town, and the man stomped off.

Nick, with one arm around Oscar, the other around Rachel, and Jamie squeezed in between, shook his head and said, "I love nineteenth-century justice. Thank you, Josiah."

Josiah put his hand on Oscar's head and smiled. "Just doing the right thing, Nick, just doing the right thing."

"You're coming to the wedding tomorrow, aren't you, Josiah?" asked Rachel.

"You bet'cha. I wouldn't miss it for the world!"